THE TRAGEDY OF FIDEL CASTRO

THE TRAGEDY OF FIDEL CASTRO

João Cerqueira

FREIGHT BOOKS

First published in 2015
Freight Books
49-53 Virginia Street
Glasgow, G1 1TS
www.freightbooks.co.uk

A CIP catalogue reference for this book is available from the British Library

ISBN 9781910449226
eISBN 9781910449233

Typeset by Freight in Plantin
Printed and bound in by Bell & Bain Ltd, Glasgow

the publisher acknowledges investment from
Creative Scotland toward the publication of this book

João Cerqueira has a PhD in History of Art from the University of Oporto. He had four year research sponsorship grant awarded by the Portuguese Science and Technology Foundation (FCT), within the field of history of art. He covered the Porto 2001 European Capital of Culture for Arte IbÈrica magazine. He is the author of seven books including *Art and Literature in the Spanish Civil War, Blame It On Too Much Freedom, The Tragedy of Fidel Castro* (winner of the Beverly Hills Book Prize and USA Book Prize) and *Devil's Observations*. This the first UK publication of *The Tragedy of Fidel Castro*.

FOREWORD

This book takes place in an imaginary time and space. All characters and organisations mentioned are entirely fictional.

Hence, Christ has nothing to do with Jesus Christ, the son of God, born in the year 0 and crucified by the Romans 33 years later.

God does not represent God, the creator of the world and men, as no one has ever been able to depict Him.

JFK is someone other than an American president with the same initials.

Fátima has no connection whatsoever with a particular site in Portugal where, it is claimed, a miracle once occurred.

Fidel Castro perhaps has some similarities with the revolutionary leader and dictator, Fidel Castro. All the other characters, in principle, never existed.

PROLOGUE

After the second ring, God answered the phone and heard a woman's anxious voice. 'Master, it's me. The war's about to begin.'

'Oh, for God's sake!' exclaimed God in exasperation.

Fátima, expecting to hear a philosophical tirade or, at the very least, some potent theological parable, retorted ironically, 'Well, that's the world for you!'

God pretended he had nothing to do with what went on down there, but realising he had let down his disciple, he tried to make amends: 'One day I shall send my son to Earth again, but when I do, it will be to give them a good hiding.'

Fátima, not averse to administering the occasional reprimand, cheered up a little. 'He's the only one who could prevent a tragedy.'

God, feeling challenged to demonstrate his omnipotence once more, snapped his fingers *click!*, and there it was. He realised he had to act. His irritation gave way to annoyance (hadn't he given proof enough?). 'I'll do what I can, but I'm not promising anything.'

Before talking to his son, who, according to the celestial gossips, had been in a bad mood lately, God, feeling pensive, decided to pray a little – in Latin, so his prayers would be more effective. Then, feeling his soul reinvigorated, he went up to Christ's living quarters and knocked gently at the door. 'May I come in?'

Christ, still in good shape after his resuscitation, was immune to the angelic slander (which was typical of beings that don't even piss or know what sex they are). Radiating goodwill and kindness, he welcomed God with a smile.

'I already know what you want me to do.'

'Do you?'

'Of course. Ever since I came up to Heaven, I've been omniscient too.'

'Well, then. Don't you want to go down and instil some order into that mob? You know I'm not going to have any more kids at my age.'

No, I don't. Once was quite enough. Goodness knows what they'd do to me this time.'

'Are you afraid they wouldn't recognise you, that you'd be outshone by the new idols?'

Christ was offended at this and sulked a little. After all, he was a beautiful man, dark, with blue eyes and an athletic build, and had been depicted in paintings and on calendars by artists who had never set eyes on him. A crystalline silence rose heavenward. Two cherubs ventured a few chords on their harps to relieve the tension, but they were blasted by a glare from the Almighty and withdrew in a flutter of poultry wings. Finally, afraid that he'd been too sarcastic, God tried praising his son: 'Almost everyone loves you, you know. Even those who don't believe in you admire you. You're a benchmark for the whole of humanity!'

Having shifted the responsibility – that ancient cross – onto Christ's shoulders, God, who liked to delegate so as to observe conflicts from a distance, accurately anticipated his boy's decision.

Christ, knowing that one shouldn't argue with one's parents since they are only concerned with one's own good – even when it doesn't seem like it, past experience has disproved it, or the future does not advise it – realised that there was only one Saviour. 'Alright, I'll go. But let's wait a bit to see how they behave.'

At this God smiled, as only the gods are able to smile, and lit up the heavens.

I

JFK

Wandering through the muddy fairground with two guardsmen, JFK watched the seething commercial activity exultantly. Here were buyers and sellers from all parts of the world, including from the land of Fidel. To these he would close his eyes and open his purse strings. Business was business and it was not worth spoiling everything for the sake of politics. The language of trade was pure – numbers, dollar signs, percentages – immune to ethical or ideological corruption. That's how it had always been and how it would remain. It was not up to him to question the morality of the system, because, ultimately, the fault lay with the principles and values that had failed to adapt to economic developments. Between paralysing rigidity and dynamic flexibility, the choice was an easy one to make.

In secret, bold merchants would offer JFK the enemy's best cigars, receiving in exchange some demijohns of bourbon from the demarcated regions for Fidel. These transactions were the only link between the two leaders, and were as consistent as the animosity that separated them. At Christmas, each sent the other luxury gifts in a Cold War–style competition designed to impress the enemy. The last case of puros sent by El Comandante had been of exceptional quality. Far superior to the bourbon I sent him, JFK reflected, puffing the warm smoke.

As he watched the mercantile bustle, musically accompanied by the crystalline tinkle of coins, he felt a great pride in the economic vitality of his country. Whenever he compared it with Fidel's fragile economy, artificially bolstered by the state, he was overcome with patriotic raptures. He found it inconceivable how the Castro regime could ban free enterprise, thereby wasting the opportunity to tax the rich, an art that required considerable effort and imagination, admittedly. And he found it harder to believe that the state also undertook all the population's needs when there was clearly not enough money for it. Fidel obviously hasn't the slightest notion about human nature, he ruminated. That urge to mollycoddle the poor seemed to him both naïve and pedantic.

His economic system worked much better: the reward incentive was the engine of society and put everyone in their rightful place. Though, of course, some, like himself, had seats that had been reserved. Nevertheless, when he saw the unbridled greed of some of the new Pharisees, he would reflect apprehensively on the warnings issued by his counsellor, who stoutly defended more state regulation: 'Their fatherland is their capital; give them freedom but never let them loose.'

Mingling with the people, listening to the miracle cures promised by evangelical pastors, he came across a group of penitents trudging aimlessly along. These were converted criminals, repentant prostitutes, famished wretches, blind men, and cripples. Prayers disintegrating into terrifying moans composed nightmarish melodies, which, in the darkness of night would return amplified to the ears of all who heard them. Each seemed bent on proving that he had the most serious flaws or owed the most splendid favour. The sight of this group disturbed the people, unleashing the demons they harbored within. It was not the madness they feared so much as the accusing blast that would ignite the crackling hellfire of guilt. Even so, morbid curiosity would still draw them toward this spectacle of dementia.

Though accustomed to man's brutal attempts to win divine recognition, JFK couldn't help but feel uneasy as he stared at the grotesque scene of those that had escaped illness or who imagined themselves to have committed unforgiveable sins. How far can man's folly go? he wondered. Some priests told him that madness was the sign of the presence of the demon, though others claimed it was a divine blessing, which made him wonder who, in the end, was truly insane.

However, some of his ruminations were more pragmatic: What if someone convinces them that they are not to blame, rather those who govern them? What if a new Fidel Castro appears to incite them to rebellion? What if Judgement Day gives rise to settling scores on earth? What will happen? Tormented with anxiety, he imagined the people rising up against him, peasants brandishing hoes, his house burned.

JFK was not afraid to confront the army of El Comandante. What he feared most was the subversive message: the emancipation of the masses, their awakening from lethargy, the growing awareness of their own power.

As the president, he was only one man, and there were no more than a few dozen generals. But the people, his soldiers included, consisted of millions of men and women. His country's greatness lay in his ability to harness this powerful collective force and use it to clear the steep paths to glory.

But, from time to time, evil beings would appear that were more dangerous than any army. These supreme threats manifested in the form of men of faith or warriors, both of whom wielded words like weapons, words that would shake the people out of their torpor, breaking the spell. Once awake, that famished beast would turn on its masters, devouring them. He knew that he was standing on a dormant volcano that sooner or later would erupt, sending a sizzling jet of lava in his direction. But his Pompeii was surely still far off. The darkness protects us; they will go on hating themselves as long as they stay in the shadows, he reflected, gazing at the band of penitents.

Nonetheless, the unending conflict with Fidel was exhausting him, leaving him lost in a labyrinth of strategies doomed to failure. As soon as a new idea occurred to him, he would ruthlessly reject it, unmasking some blocked reasoning. Wherever his mind led him, he would come to a dead end and have to start over. Each time that happened, he grew more tired. He would then recall his numerous military victories and the diplomatic skill he would use whenever force was unadvisable; there were so many powerful men who had been brought low by his strength, astuteness, or gold coins. Recalling his past glories always filled him with pride and renewed confidence. It was his opium. The euphoria would wear off minutes later, however, and anguish would return. He continued along the fairground paths and through the crossroads of reasoning, yearning for inspiration to end the exhausting conflict with Fidel.

A gust of wind shook his coat and icily caressed his neck. JFK shivered and found himself alone. He was staring into the abyss that people call the sky, gaping at the sheer size of it. It confused him to try to conceive of its beginning, and he didn't dare imagine its end. At that moment he understood that his nation was no more than a splinter off an infinite universe and his own existence merely a brief flash in the tremendous cosmic darkness.

He felt lost and wondered if God had abandoned him.

As night gradually settled over the day, composing delicate hybrid hues, he glimpsed the mansion of J. E. Hoover and stopped instinctively. He had heard terrible tales about this sinister figure ever since he was a child: stories of drinking animal blood and biting off birds' heads, all invented by his nanny to make him eat his soup. Now, though, J. E. Hoover was his main ally. Yet for some, Hoover wielded more power than the president, thanks to a vast network of informers and spies constantly supplying him with compromising information about the country's citizens. It was said that Hoover kept detailed files that could destroy anyone's reputation, including that of JFK, that he had ordered phones to be hacked, and that he had access to confidential legal information. For that very reason, it was claimed, Hoover had the generals, clergy, bourgeoisie, and wise men all in his hand, each of them hostages to scandal.

Although he would callously berate Fidel Castro, burning up in ire like Cato recalling Carthage, Hoover's most exquisite hatred was reserved for the counsellor. This was partly because of his importance to JFK, as if the deference shown to him obliterated part of what was due to himself. But it was also because he had never found anything in the counsellor's conduct − not sex, nor drugs, nor drink − that could be used to mire him in shame. He had no trumps with which to manipulate him.

For a few moments, JFK remained before J. E. Hoover's house with a strange taste of cabbage soup in his mouth. He recalled Hoover's words during the last Council of State: 'Human beings have an innate taste for servitude and subservience, a strange resignation to abuse, which allows minorities to tame the masses without much effort. That is why those who promise to emancipate them also throw them into the dungeons, as if it were the same thing. This is the reality, the only social contract possible. Let us not generate needs in them of which they are unaware, nor appetites for which we might one day become the food. The people are ugly, dirty, and bad, and all they want is bread and circuses.'

JFK was in session with the counsellor, and both kept a meditative silence. JFK began to pace around the table, closely imitated by his counsellor.

Seen from above, through the reticulated eyes of a fly on the ceiling, these moving bodies would be transfigured into two masses of different shapes and sizes − a large rectangular one in front and a small spherical one behind. Such was the synchrony that as soon as one slowed his pace, the other would immediately follow suit. Likewise, any increase in speed would instantly be matched. However, as concord between two men never lasts long, JFK switched direction and crashed into the counsellor, sending him flying some six feet − according to the mental calculations of the fly on the ceiling.

'Careful!' shouted JFK, rubbing his belly. 'I've had an idea,' said the counsellor, prostrate. JFK pricked up his ears. Then, as he'd once seen in a play at the theatre, the counsellor got up and moved to the window. With his back to the president, he asked, 'Mister President, how can you tell the strength and weakness of a man?'

'Well…'

'To defeat Fidel we have to get into his mind, learn to think like he thinks, feel as he feels.'

'What if we turn into communists too?'

'Don't worry, there's a man that can help us – Castro's spy, captured last year. All you have to do is question him about his ideological concepts, his faith in the revolution, and the hatred he feels for our model of society. In other words, just let the tape play on to the end, and you'll decipher the mindset of his mentor.'

Without bothering to summon guardsmen, JFK and the counsellor headed straight to the cell to interrogate the man who could unlock doors into the intricate mind of Fidel Castro. In his eagerness for quick answers, JFK broke into a gallop that forced the counsellor to run to keep up with him.

'I have one small doubt, counsellor. How are we going to make him talk?'

'We are going to earn his trust, seduce him.'

'Wouldn't it be better to use more traditional methods, already tried and tested?'

The cells were located near the river in an occupied building, once a cosmopolitan cultural centre. Facing westward, the rectangular building had a central open courtyard, three floors, and a two-gabled roof whose garrets had been converted into lookout posts for the sentries. The façades were broken by large, barred windows, and there was a single doorway, equipped with a heavy knocker. Bathed in dusky light, the stones emitted warm tones and fiery reflections shone in the windows. Glowing gently as if a profound mystical charge were emanating from it, the lockup seemed more like a place of repose and meditation. JFK and the counsellor contemplated it. Like an apparition, the building radiated dazzling light, which held their gaze. 'What Fidel would give for a prison like this!' burbled JFK, quite numb with aesthetic ecstasy. Stunned, the counsellor closed his eyes.

At the door, JFK hesitated politely. 'Do you not think it might be a bit late to visit?'

'They're still up. Anyway, it's your prison.'

Not wishing to be rude, JFK gently tapped on the wood with the metal knocker. Knock, knock.

'Who's there?' yelled an uncouth, ill-humoured voice.

'Us!'

'Us who?'

'Me, JFK, and the counsellor.'

'Got your ID?'

Irritated by the ignorance and unwillingness of servants, all too common in public services, the counsellor roared: 'If you don't open the door immediately, we shall have you hung before the day is out!'

The heavy door swung open, letting out a squeal of pain, such was the effort upon its poor old joints. A billow of musty air smacked them in the face like spittle, as if it had been waiting for the chance to escape.

'Would you be so kind as to step this way, Mister President?'

A ragged cloak, stretched out on the porch, served as a red carpet for the guests. Planted on it, looking sleepy and forcing a smile was the prison governor. Opening his arms, he greeted JFK effusively: 'Mister President, to what do we owe this honor?' JFK recoiled. He could well dispense with such excesses of affection, which would only give him lice and scabies.

'We've come on a top-secret mission. All I can say is that we wish to interrogate Fidel's spy.'

'But that's against the rules!'

'Who do you think makes the rules if not the president?'

snapped the counsellor, restoring the logic of hierarchy.

'Well, in our land, rules were not made to be kept, were they?' quipped the governor, feeling that his authority was being undermined.

'Take us to him, O scrupulous servant of the nation,' bade JFK.

The former cinema, theatre, and conference hall had been converted into collective cells, while the remaining rooms of the old cultural centre served as dormitories for the wardens, a canteen, workshop, library, and the governor's quarters. For one hour a day, all prisoners were let loose in the courtyard to get some sun. They usually passed the time kicking each other violently as they pretended to be playing football.

All, that was, except Varadero, Fidel Castro's spy, who had been placed in top-security solitary confinement. 'We can't let him mix with the other prisoners, or he'll start converting them to the revolution and then there'll be trouble,' explained the governor. 'Because of him, two dangerous criminals have taken to using berets and smoking cigars, while another has been greeting people with a clenched fist without so much as a by-your-leave. The cooks have been heckling for a raise and the guards have set up a labour committee. If I hadn't taken measures, goodness knows where it might have led.'

'I see, I see,' said JFK pensively.

'One day, we had a riot among the prisoners because he decided to organise criticism and self-criticism sessions, and they all took advantage of it to set upon each other and complain.'

'That man's a danger,' said JFK.

The governor decided to take the opportunity to give them a guided tour of the establishment. 'Before I take you to see the spy, I'm going to show you the main cell, where we keep the most dangerous thugs on the face of the earth,' he declared importantly, trying to boost his own worth. As they passed, the strip of light projected by the torches transformed the three men into distorted shadows that slid along the walls in a two-dimensional procession. In this journey into darkness, strange phenomena occurred, turning the counsellor into a giant and causing JFK and the governor to sometimes blend into a single patch with undefined contours. And thus the three flesh-and-blood beings and the phantasmagoric figures that accompanied them proceeded abreast down a long corridor until they arrived at a large collective cell, the former theatre.

Its new actors had arranged themselves across the existing space, now bereft of seats. Some were standing, others seated, almost all involved in dialogues that ranged in tone from excitement to serenity, intense gesticulations to sleepy quietness, as if the stage director had allowed them total freedom to express themselves in a rehearsal without beginning or end. In scenes of greatest emotional intensity, groups of various sizes raised their voices and pushed and shoved at each other as if in a prelude to a brawl. In more intimate scenes, two or three men murmured confidences or told fantastic stories, while one or two solitary actors uttered seemingly interminable soliloquies.

Free of rules, logical sequence, or common thread, the plot changed every day. Thus, the madmen of the last rehearsal, who had been writhing on the ground trying to strangle each other, were now given minor roles and sat quietly in the corner playing dice. Characters who, till then, had displayed a remarkable inner peace and serenity were now overcome with a sudden, inexplicable fury, causing them to bang their heads against the walls. It was as if each man was determined to discover the role he could play to perfection, and he pursued that goal single-mindedly. In today's preparations, many of the actors were competing for the main roles, provoking their companions with insults or deliberately bumping into them. This type of rehearsal often coincided with the days of intense heat, which seemed to originate in the theatre room, urging the play toward a violent tragic end.

Suffocating in the stifling atmosphere, the room seemed to pant with the effort and dripped beads of sweat from its ceiling. Insects on the verge of incineration fled from the bowels of the earth into the performance, ending up crushed by bare feet. The theatre then seemed like an obsolete boiler about to burst, having been forced to work beyond its capacities. The passion was reaching boiling point.

This was how the turbulent rehearsal was running when JFK, the counsellor, and the prison governor arrived at the barred door. The actors were exceeding themselves as if this was the last show they would ever do and gilt statuettes had been promised them. Suddenly, the hubbub drained away with a confused whine, such as might be produced by an out-of-tune instrument, as if the voices had been sucked back into the actors' throats.

The room filled with silence.

'Mister President has honoured us with his presence,' called the governor, with his hands clasped behind his back, standing on tiptoe to make himself look more important. 'Give us a few words, your excellency: say something to the people here.' The governor winked at JFK.

'You speak, counsellor, go on,' whispered JFK in alarm.

'Me?'

'Yes, quick!'

Taken by surprise, the counsellor decided to say something he believed to be sensible and educational for such men. 'Er… his excellency has asked me to pronounce the following words: at this time of deprivation and suffering, you should take the opportunity to reflect carefully on that precious commodity called freedom, which no treasure in the world can ever replace. Use the time available to you to instruct and educate yourselves so that, when you return to life in society, you can improve your living conditions through your own merits, and thus escape the vicious cycle of poverty and crime.' A dig in the ribs from the governor caused the counsellor's face to gnarl in a grimace of pain, and he stopped speaking abruptly.

'Mister President, this man is a communist! I'm going to arrest him immediately,' growled the governor. The counsellor hid behind JFK.

'Wait! He's got problems… too much work, marital trouble, stuff like that,' explained JFK.

'I can recognise a communist when I see one,' replied the governor. Veins were bulging in his eyes and the hairs on his nose stood on end.

'So can I, so can I. That's why I assure you he's innocent.'

'I'm telling you, he's a communist!'

'No, he's not!'

'Yes, he is!'

'No, he's not!'

'Yes, he is!'

'Shut up!'

Another one for the blacklist, thought the governor, obediently nodding agreement with JFK.

Varadero was surprised by the unexpected visit of the three men, particularly as one of them was the mythical leader of the enemy nation he had been taught to hate. Given the sound of approaching footsteps on the flagstones, he could feel that something unusual was about to happen. Since the prisoner had been deprived of a view of any events taking place outside his cell, his ears had begun to function like radar, detecting suspicious movements and then transforming them through the exercise of a rational imagination into more-or-less plausible hypotheses. Thus, he began constructing another reality whose raw material was extracted by his ears, which penetrated the confines of the prison like a miner digging deep into the bowels of the earth. Having obtained the necessary material, the work of edification was taken over by the brain, with the imagination acting as the architect that invents forms, and his reason as the engineer that makes sure the building will stand. This partnership naturally gave rise to some conflicts, as the architect was prone to soaring flights of fancy which the pragmatic engineer could not keep up with. Thus, hardly had the vibration of the first footsteps resounded on Varadero's eardrums than his fantasy began to expand, floating ungoverned until it came up against the solid walls of reason.

It is El Comandante himself who has come to save me. He is making the governor crawl along at his feet.

Then he questioned his musing. Don't you think that if it were El Comandante, there would have been shots and explosions, and the prisoners would all be cheering him as their liberator?

So…?

So maybe they've come to shoot you.

Much of his uncertainty dissipated when the door of his cell fell open. Varadero recoiled in astonishment.

JFK and the counsellor gazed at him in fascination, as if he were an extraterrestrial, a prehistoric creature, a clone, or, indeed, a Castro spy. The governor felt increasingly important.

'I'm ready, you wretches,' growled the prisoner, listening to his more rational side.

'No one is going to hurt you, spy,' said JFK. 'We only want to talk to you.'

'You won't get a single word out of me.'

'The best thing is to hang him upside down, Mister President.'

Realising that the meeting had gotten off to a bad start, and knowing the importance of first impressions, the counsellor intervened diplomatically. 'We have come to invite you to take a walk.'

'Don't even think about it,' the voices of Varadero and the governor collided.

So JFK decided to remind them just who was in charge and how to exercise power in delicate situations. 'Dear servant of the nation, I am most grateful to you for having brought us to this man, who seems to be very well treated, something which certainly would not have happened if one of our spies had been thrown into a dungeon in his country. But now, leave him to us. Go mind your own business.'

Having managed to contain his first fit of fury, the governor was still struggling with the second as he shot down the corridors like a bullet. 'It was that communist dwarf that ruined him!'

Once more, three men paced the corridor, this time in the opposite direction, with Varadero taking the governor's place. Their phantasmagoric shadows caressed the insensitive walls, with the counsellor again becoming a grotesque giant and JFK and Varadero blending together in a shapeless, black mass.

When they reached the end no one was waiting at the door to pay homage to them. The offended governor had chosen to disregard the rules of hierarchy and etiquette and had returned to his office in a sulk. To take his mind off the royal snub, he rechecked the data he meticulously collected about the prison population. No one has been hanged this month, he reflected, with a heavy conscience. Earlier, however, he had sent a messenger to J. E. Hoover.

JFK's sportsman arm, muscular from numerous fights, managed to fling his stone a good hundred metres out to sea. Varadero's spy arm, hard from cutting sugar cane, flung his about the same distance. In that Cold War competition, each player would occasionally shoot a glance at the other, the expression somewhere between curiosity and admiration. Despite being aware of the implicit turn-taking rule, at one point they threw their pebbles at exactly the same time, with both lumps of rock flying side-by-side until they crashed into the foam of a wave. A collective 'Sorry' was uttered equally simultaneously. Then, still on uncertain ground, similar to the consistency of the sand on which they were walking, their conversation advanced, step-by-step.

Tired of stone skipping, and fed-up with always coming in last in that game, the counsellor picked up some words and threw them with much more skill than he had the stones. 'What's your name?'

'Varadero.'

'I'm the counsellor.'

'And I'm JFK.'

Each of them began to wonder what should be said next.

Having cultivated a relaxed, almost trusting atmosphere, thanks to the charms of a moonlit beach and the childish game – the stones in that case serving to bond the men instead of cracking open their skulls – no one wanted to spoil it by making an innocent blunder. Even Varadero felt the pressure to say something. As a result, there was a new wave of silence, heavier than the one before, which not even stones could break.

So they began to scrutinise the firmament in the hope of spotting a falling star, comet, or maybe even a mysterious flying object. But no suitable topic of conversation occurred to them. It was as if they needed to find the right poetry to seduce a damsel, and struck dumb, could not find it, the brain paralysed when most needed.

Then, stiltedly, each word coming forth at great cost to his mouth, then bursting out in a final bid to be free, JFK let loose the following observation: 'I suppose you must miss your homeland very much.' The phrase, apparently naïve, was the catalyst that untied Varadero's tongue, the supreme goal of this innocent nocturnal stroll on the beach.

Taken by surprise, not knowing if this was an insult or a compliment, the spy let the blow enter him and waited a few seconds for the consequences of the impact. Strangely enough, a pleasant sensation grew in his chest and then expanded to the rest of his body, culminating in deeper, slower breathing. His smile, which had been imprisoned since his detention, burst free of its shackles. Then he began to speak.

'I come from an island of heat, happiness, and beautiful women. However, it is not those features that distinguish my world from yours. In my country, the exploiters and the exploited have given way to a classless society where the state acts for the common good. Our model of scientific socialism generates abundance and allows each citizen to develop his human potential. It is therefore a much more developed state than your decrepit capitalist society based on the selfishness of a minority that exploits the workers.'

'If it's so marvellous, then why do so many try to escape on rafts?' enquired the counsellor ironically, sensing a chance to shine with cutting remarks after his stone-skipping failure.

'Will you be quiet? Let the gentleman speak,' said JFK sharply.

'In your world, man is alienated from what he produces, transformed into a mere commodity to be bought and sold. To keep prices low, you have created an army of unemployed, thanks to laws that encourage dismissal.'

'Is that so? And where people with PhDs drive taxis, not to mention the pros—'

'Don't interrupt him, idiot!'

'You have invented a god to console yourselves against the miseries of life, opium for the masses, but what you truly venerate is money. Your modern saints are the wealthy. People that do good deeds and philanthropic acts are not admired, only those that get rich. And in their eagerness to imitate those vultures, people trample over each other furiously and commit scurrilous acts, transforming human relations into a merciless struggle where the strong triumph and impose their laws. On the other hand, knowing how humiliation can generate profit, you encourage them to debase themselves in exchange for money. Dignity and the sense of the ridiculous have also been bought—'

'So you've finally got something right.'

'Shh!'

'To keep the system going, the great capitalists also have to control the laws, which they manage to do by financing the parties that will govern, so that they, in turn, will pass laws in accordance with their interests and not in the interests of the majority. And when the tentacles of capital stretch to the legislation of a country then the nation is completely subordinated, manipulated to do its bidding. Thus the circle is closed, with capitalism forming a natural continuation of slavery and feudalism.'

'Our system may have its flaws, but what incentives does

your system offer to encourage people to work?' This time JFK, believing the question to be a pertinent one, did not admonish the counsellor.

'Incentives? That's your big problem—' (Varadero had almost called them 'friends.') 'Everything is reduced to the logic of capital – it takes over your souls and you are incapable of conceiving life outside it. But what is the result? A patient that cannot pay for his treatment is left to die, which means that in capitalism, whoever doesn't have money is not only scorned by most of society, but is also condemned to capital punishment. Counsellor, our incentives are different: to collaborate in the construction of a society grounded in solidarity to build a new world where the sun shines on all, to reach the last phase of the march of history and create paradise on earth.'

'That all sounds very nice in theory,' said the counsellor.

'But it can only be put into practice through revolution, with workers taking up arms to overthrow their oppressors.'

'Oh, yes, that will happen, you can be sure of it! But perhaps it won't happen where you think it will, nor take the form you expect,' retorted the counsellor, taking pleasure in his enigmatic sarcasm.

'Under the command of Fidel, our people overthrew a corrupt regime and installed a unique social model under which all citizens enjoy the same rights and opportunities,' Varadero continued, indifferent to the counsellor.

'Tell me, Varadero, now that you have lived some time in our society, do you really believe it is inferior to yours?' asked JFK, engrossed in the debate.

The spy took his time to reply, entwining his hands and then pressing the fingers of his right hand against those of the left, feeling a blind knot in his tendons. 'Well, in fact, there are one or two dialectic contradictions that we have not yet managed to sort out.'

'Rule of law, private property, one man, one vote?' suggested the counsellor.

The sea was a dark mantle shaken by the winds and whims of the moon, and in it floated the naked bodies of the three men. The undulations moved convulsively, rocking them in an irregular rhythm. In the aquatic immensity they were mere playthings. Floating on his back, the counsellor stared at the winking stars, feeling as if he were gliding among them. Varadero challenged the waves, offering his chest for them to break against. JFK kicked the weever fish.

'Shall we bathe?' the spy had said.

The boat had weighed anchor at dawn, the sun behind it illuminating the way like a lighthouse. Glittering sparks ignited and fizzled out in the water. The keel cut through the sea, its blunt blade leaving a linear scar that instantly regenerated. Restored, the sea took revenge on the hull of the ship, battering it continuously with violent blows that aggravated old wounds. The boat's mechanical metabolism caused it to spew out oil and burnt fuel. Fish, dissatisfied with how the boat was fouling their environment, leapt out of the water, trying in vain to take flight. To the relief of these fish, but the disappointment of the seagulls and albatrosses, this was not a fishing boat. In its hold, for the exclusive delectation of the revolutionary elite, were barrels of bourbon, televisions, perfumes, and a crate full of Statue of Liberty miniatures.

The captain of the boat was an accepted smuggler, who, like all professionals in his line of business, was respected, decorated, and commended. This was a journey he made every week, and he boasted that it was so boring he could sail to any of his destinations with his eyes shut. However, this crossing was different from the others. On the prow, standing, his passenger anxiously scanned the line of the horizon. In his imagination, he had already landed long ago on that island that could not yet be discerned in the sea mist.

'Why did you let him go?'

'Human beings are the product of their circumstances, counsellor.'

II

FIDEL CASTRO

Colourful colonial mansions, flaunted arches, verandas, and balustrades. Abandoned houses bombarded by time. Impervious concrete blocks. Buses crammed full of people. Tall, strong, agile bodies and heavy, slow, flaccid ones, all waiting for the carriage of history that had already passed. Cars straight out of museums, propelled by magic and miracles of maintenance. Marxist cars devoid of charm and efficiency. Cavalcades of bicycles making their way silently up long avenues. Hot wind. Waves breaking against the sea wall. Eyes lost on the horizon. Chess players in the square absorbed in abstract reasoning. Arguments about *pelota tiene lógica*. The *guarapo* vendor massacring the sugar cane to extract the juice that looked like dirty dishwater. Cockroaches crawling and cockroaches flying. Cockroach carcasses on the sidewalk. Lethal gas to kill them with. Pharmacies empty of medicines, attesting to exemplary levels of public health. The heat of the sun transformed into musical notes. Uninterrupted dance. Cheap rooms to let. Tropical sex. Sexual tourism. Sweat. Tremendous electric storms. Flooding. Swimming cockroaches. Tired lamps going out one by one. Optimistic television news. Clandestine restaurants. Swordfish steaks with black beans. Mojitos and daiquiris. Public praise and private insults. Security guards keeping watch. Unspeakable escape plans. An old soldier sitting forgotten in a doorway, eyeing the tourists sowing banknotes. Searing passions. Unknown languages. Piles of rare books for sale, all on the same subject. Children in white and red uniforms, guaranteeing the future of the revolution.

The meeting of the Central Committee was about to start. The room was tense with expectations about what Fidel Castro would say. This time it was not so much the length of the speech that was feared as its content, because, as rumour had it, it was going to be different from usual. A final war against the nation of JFK was imminent, and everyone feared a new invasion attempt, a new blockade, or – worse – a ceasefire declaration from the enemy, a request for peace. 'Then who would we blame for our troubles?' people muttered darkly under their breath. The situation was dramatic. Fidel had already survived near-fatal crises and had escaped from the tightest spots. But this time he was facing the biggest threat to the revolution since he had driven out the former dictator.

Sitting at the centre of the table, in a haze of aromatic smoke, he was nostalgically recalling the days immediately after he had seized power – his dramatic descent from the mountains, the mass support of the peasants, the dictator's forces effortlessly overcome, his triumphant entry into the capital like an envoy from the heavens (indeed, many had seen him as such), delirious crowds, the improvised rallies, a dove perched on his shoulder, revolutionary euphoria sweeping across the whole island. Everything had been possible back then and everything seemed like it was going to get done: the reconstruction of a country by the practical application of a utopian ideology; the nationalisation of lands, houses, and businesses; agrarian reform; literacy and health campaigns; the founding of schools and hospitals; the promotion of sport; a ban on gambling and prostitution; settling of accounts; persecutions, trials, and convictions; *el paredón*[1]. His life was

---

1. Firing squad

drawing to an end, and the film of all those important events was constantly running in his mind.

So much done, yet so much left to do.

Fidel had closely monitored all the stages of the revolution, each project started and each project abandoned, showing the way along a road that he himself had constructed and destroyed. This had once been a great highway that had aroused the admiration of other builders and travellers, but today it was a dirt track full of potholes that petered out on the brink of the abyss. Despite this – or perhaps because of it – he had isolated himself more and more as time went by, discovering that the pleasures and frustrations of power are something best savoured alone, like a *puro*. That vice had grown uncontrollable.

Cooled by a giant fan hanging over his head with blades like the sword of Damocles, ready to decapitate him at one false word, the Central Committee's rapporteur began reading out data on the state of the nation.

'This year, like last year, our performance has been magnificent, and our rigorous and accurate planning has brought great development. The figures are not really important. What interests us is the people's commitment and the amazing results achieved through their enthusiastic efforts. They have once more demonstrated their unconditional support for the Revolution. Having no profit is the most emphatic way of rejecting capitalism. The bourgeois property-owners dream of amassing wealth, but we revolutionaries will not tire until we have destroyed it.'

As the rapporteur read, Fidel listened with apprehension, anticipating the grating sound each phrase would produce in his ears. It generated a muffled rattle in the slow-moving carousel in his head. Only the sound of his own voice could bring him silence.

'It is, for all of us, a great joy to see how the revolution is progressing and to learn of our people's ever-growing commitment to this ongoing enterprise. For although there have been attempts at sabotage and terrorist attacks by our many enemies, although we have few resources available and nature has been hard on us, our great work remains alive, setting a unique example for the oppressed peoples of the world.' The audience prepared for the first of many rounds of applause that would rhythmically punctuate Fidel's speech. Then suddenly, overcoming the more objectionable fantasies, he changed direction. Abandoning the triumphant tone, he admitted that not all was well. 'While all this is scientific fact, it is nevertheless necessary to point out that our economy has a few problems that we have been unable to solve. The traditional methods have proved ineffective. It has therefore become imperative to find new ways of confronting JFK.'

At this point, there was a visible contraction inside the room, as if the company, like a group of terrified apprentices afraid of being interrogated by their implacable master, was trying to shield itself from hard questions by forming a solid mass. Fidel shot them with his eyes till they dropped dead from sheer fear. Finally, having aimed at everyone present, he fired again. This time, he launched a more powerful and deadly weapon, prohibited by international revolutionary conventions. 'We have only one alternative left. And though this might seem at first sight like a betrayal of the revolution, a capitulation to the laws of capitalism, the denial of everything that has been done till now, in fact it is only a temporary measure, a small matter of dialectical fine-tuning. From now on, I declare the island open to international tourism!'

To say that a lightning bolt hit the Central Committee room would be an understatement. The delegates (with the thunderbolt still in their heads) stared at Fidel Castro, outraged. Accustomed to the world's criticism, hardened by taunts and gibes, Fidel shrugged this off and calmly lit another cigar, *Cohiba Siglo XXI*. With the first puff, he sent out a cloud of smoke that obfuscated the tenuous luminosity of those that had tried to censure him. Not content with this, he fired a second gas attack, which provoked fits of coughing and caused eyes to become itchy and red, as red as the revolution was rapidly ceasing to be.

Once order had been restored to the room (in truth, it had never really left), Fidel again asserted: 'The island is now open to international tourism.' This time he even managed to drag some nods and forced smiles from those present, who were confused, like someone watching the optical illusion of a rotating wheel and wondering how an apparently backward movement could generate forward motion. But as always happens when a dogma is broken, emptiness and anguish began to lodge themselves in the hearts of the faithful. And although something new had appeared to replace it, some distrusted it and resisted. After all, they were not in the Roman Empire, where emperors would switch religion as easily as they changed their clothes until they finally got it right. In these parts, things were taken to heart, and faith was considered to be infinitely superior.

'Counter-revolutionaries and agitators will enter our country!' someone protested. Fidel didn't need to reply. His most faithful comrades, having sensed the way the wind was blowing, raised their sails, using El Comandante's ideas for support. 'Let them come. They will certainly join us, amazed at what we have achieved!'

'And how will we explain this to the people, after so many years trying to convince them that tourism is a futile bourgeois activity?'

'Let us trust in human nature, in its tendency to refuse to see what is obvious. Some will close their eyes to the matter as if nothing has happened. Others will get used to it in the end and shrug it off, as they've done up until now.'

'And what will we give them to eat? One of the bases of capitalism is gluttony, as we all know.' The debate specialists fell mute, taken aback by the subtle question.

Fidel intervened: 'There will be enough food for everyone. We will counteract the excesses and obesity of the capitalists by imposing a new diet on our people that will give them the trimmest figures ever seen.'

Not satisfied with this, the sceptical launched a new wave of impertinent questions, frothing with doubts. 'And what will they say about the run-down state of our architectural heritage?'

'Don't you know that all ancient monuments are ruins? The more decayed they are, the better.'

'And will we have to work out tourist routes, allow the multinationals to build hotels on revolutionary soil?'

'The best way of defeating our enemies is to infiltrate them.'

'What if the foreigners decide to take our women away with them?'

'Well, first of all, we've got plenty. Second, that would solve the problem of the imbalance between the population and available resources.'

'What if some of them want to settle here?'

'That would be definitive proof that capitalism is now in its final phase.'

As no one dared ask any more questions, even though the explanations had been unconvincing, Fidel spoke again. 'Our beaches and our tropical sun are the future foundations of the revolution.' The person who said that was a great communist writer persecuted by the bourgeoisie, who predicted the solution to our problems while also pointing out the unsolvable failures of the capitalist system.' Fidel picked up an old book with a yellowed cover and began to read aloud some passages, skipping lines when it suited him.

'The countryside and the beach, the mountain air and the sea air, are effectively a universal panacea for the great afflictions endemic to large cities... for the patients of all abuses of work and pleasure... the absorbing concerns... of money, ambition, glory... all this together, let me tell you, slowly eats away at the foundations of the human organism, gradually corroding it and causing it to become unbalanced and degenerate.'[2]

This time, although the delegates silently continued to think up curses and insults against tourism and against Fidel himself, they felt themselves being transcended by something. Some, impressed by the commandant's shrewdness and the words of the communist prophet, realised their own shortsightedness and were overcome with an intense feeling of shame. They had never heard those words, nor of the author, another significant flaw to confess at the next criticism and self-criticism session. Feeling humbled and small, they again cast their eyes to the ground, abashed. Fidel did not have to use his weapons on them again.

Worthy of a final judgment, this collective repentance session indicated a drawn-out purgatory. If they were not materialist atheists, the delegates would perhaps be on their knees praying to a redemptive divinity, intoning psalms and chastising themselves. *That was easier than I thought,* Fidel reflected. *None of these idiots could ever replace me, that's for sure!*

Then, to redeem the penitents, or perhaps just to get the matter over and done with, he brought the meeting to a conclusion. 'With the introduction of tourism, we will solve three serious problems in one fell swoop. Foreign currency will flow into our coffers, which will allow us to confront JFK, and perhaps most important of all, we will set a trap for capitalism. End of session!'

Fidel left the meeting feeling more worried than satisfied. He knew the fatal blow had been struck. His inexhaustible capacity to transform defeats into victories allowed him to play impossible tricks on the other artistes operating in the field. However, this time, the contortions had been excessive and his backbone was injured. And as there was no cure, even

---

2. ORTIGÃO, Ramalho, *As Farpas,* 5th ed. Lisboa: (Emprêsa Literária Fluminense,1926). 4, p. 247, 248.

in this wonderland of medicine, all he could do was try to limit the severity and extent of the damage. Would he ever walk upright again? That was a question he'd still not had the courage to ask himself. Right now, he was trying to assess the real consequences of tourists on the island. *What will they think of our society?* he wondered gloomily. *What image of us will they transmit to the rest of the world? How will our people react?* Meanwhile, the car with darkened windows transported him swiftly to one of his secret residences.

Fidel might also have thought, without straying very far from the truth, that it was the revolution itself that traveled inside that car, concealing itself in shame at having done something disgraceful. This was a dishonoured Revolution that was trying to escape the opprobrium it deserved, the flight from infamy dragging guilt in its wake or perhaps the guilt impelling the flight. These ruminations might have acquired an unequivocal touch of realism had the car swerved off the road into a deep ravine or been involved in a head-on collision, though in reality, nothing of this occurred.

Escaping the mesh of shantytowns surrounding the capital, the car slid rapidly toward the fields in the interior of the island, where men armed with swords battled like gladiators against unarmed sugarcanes. Exhausted, Fidel was already in the antechamber of sleep, and the film was beginning over again, the endless replay of fragments of his life that wrested him from the here-and-now and transported him into dimensions that existed only in his memory. This time he and his brother were preparing the attack on the Moncada Barracks. In the sky, a cloud was torn into tatters. The sun shone over the whole island, but its inhabitants preferred to hide in the shade.

The demonstration began as a simple conversation among a group of unemployed men gathered, as they always did, around a park bench in the capital. They were bewailing the misery of their lives in a series of complaints similar in form and content, and as usual, this was followed by the attribution of guilt. Recently, as indeed happened on this occasion, they had taken to passing sentence on the offenders and announcing their punishment.

It was common for the mercury to rise high in thermometers in those parts, but what happened next cannot really be blamed on the intense heat of the day. Other tropical countries also melted under scorching temperatures without anything of the kind taking place there. The culprits were altogether different.

We could perhaps accept that the air, dilated by the solar furnace, may have amplified the excited voices escaping from the park. This meant that, within a radius of dozens of metres, sensitive ears were able to detect unusual sound waves, which prompted eyes to search for the source and legs to execute brusque changes of direction. This concerted effort of senses and muscles resulted in a sudden influx of passers-by into the park, successive waves that gathered around the bench from where had issued the (unconscious?) appeal. At first the new members of the group just listened. But soon, they grew less tongue-tied and began to corroborate the complaints with examples from their own experience, approving the measures proposed to take justice into their own hands.

With their individuality diluted in this shapeless mass, the crowd experienced a real sense of safety and freedom that they had never known before. Let loose from the cages in which they had been born, they tried out their fragile, atrophied wings in ever more daring flights. In a short time, they were all fluttering with unrestrained fantasies that might have been graceful and serene had they not been propelled by rage, which made their movements crude and inelegant. Then, as often happens with flocks of birds lost in the sky, one member of the group suddenly swerved and headed out of the park, leading his winged companions behind him in a deafening flurry. Flying low, close to the ground, they filled the streets, attracting other stray birds to join them with a rustle of wings and voices raised in protest.

Less than an hour had passed since the start of what had

seemed like a banal conversation among friends disgruntled with the system and economic situation. However, that apparently insignificant event had swelled into a riot, and the streets of the capital were seething with demonstrators demanding reforms and changes, practically calling for the overthrow of Fidel Castro. It was as if they had been waiting for the fuse to be lit. Insolent voices shouted inflammatory words against Fidel and his government, igniting new foci of heated protest, which spread like wildfire in all directions, raising the temperature and reducing the commandant's great work to ashes. The island shook with an earthquake generated by the inhabitants themselves, a massive displacement of the human tectonic plate. Each arm raised in the air seemed bound by invisible wires to all the others, causing a surge of collective movement, while an imperceptible hiss of pain escaped from the atmosphere, pummelled by so many clenched fists.

The biblical parable about sin, sinners, and stones had long been forgotten, or its meaning distorted, as the windows of the public buildings shattered under the implacable rage of these new supporters of stoning. Never having previously sinned, immaculate in their revolutionary purity, candid in their words, acts, and omissions, they hurled anything that came to hand. The stone that hit the Havana National Theatre was the final straw, for the security forces were impatient to teach these unruly thugs a lesson. Finding their way barred by policemen and cars, the counter-revolutionaries suddenly stopped short, causing a shock wave to ripple through the long line of demonstrators, which contracted like a wounded snake. From both sides of the nonexistent barricades, threats and insults were hurled, without producing the slightest effect.

The psychological warfare would end in stalemate, a result unacceptable to either side. Change would have to be forced in a reckless bid for victory. However, neither the protestors nor the forces of law and order were sure of their own supremacy and ability to triumph; so some shouted to withdraw, while others continued clamouring to be allowed through. In the absence of any impartial referee who had the credibility and authority to resolve the dispute in another way, they all waited for the violence to erupt.

From the windows and balconies, residents who had not joined the crowd watched in silent astonishment as a phenomenon unfolded that transcended all bounds of the imagination. Something that had repeatedly been proven impossible by those who detained the truth. In another age, such an event would have been interpreted as an unequivocal sign of the end of the world, an unnatural portent that heralded the coming of the apocalypse. Indeed, a man with an elephant's head, a woman with a fishtail, or a horde of lilac dragons could not have been more convincing. Mundane reality had been ripped apart, revealing a hidden dimension; the scenery and the people were the same, but they displayed attitudes that could never have happened in a stable universe.

In fact, these new beings were behaving exactly the opposite of the inhabitants of the island, insanely breaking all rules of normal conduct. They had been brought up to believe that the revolution was the only guarantee of the common good, and they had devoted all their efforts and faith to it. The new religion was just as potent as the old and indeed the two coexisted in a kind of duplicated faith. Thus, when the terrestrial divinity was challenged, so was the celestial one. For those who managed to reinvent themselves after this unexpected metaphysical shock, they found their world had been turned inside out.

Somewhere in the process, the cogs of time got jammed.

Fidel was reclining on a sofa, lost once more in the no-man's-land between wakefulness and slumber. The film of his life begun only after the preparations for the revolution had started. Before it was only the blank space of virgin celluloid. But the spool had stuck, and the film now lingered at an unfortunate scene he had since tried unsuccessfully to erase from his mind.

It was the early years of the revolution, and the initial

consensus was beginning to fracture as the path ahead began to diverge. The mammoth task of transforming a backward society made up largely of illiterates into a model of economic development and social justice was generating different, often completely incompatible, points of view between Fidel and his closest companions. These were men who had risked their lives with him, demonstrating a remarkable courage and capacity for suffering; indeed, the deprivations of hunger, thirst, heat, and cold had created bonds between them that were apparently indestructible. Fidel respected and always listened to them attentively, discussing their ideas as long as necessary to convince them they were wrong, just as one might dissuade children from acting foolishly.

However, in recent years the tension had increased. His pronouncements, once considered infallible, were now contested; his orders, once followed to the letter, were now distorted here and there. These were small things, but they were enormous too, for they meant that each person had begun to think for himself, threatening revolutionary unity, the mainstay of the new society. Che Guevara, the eternal contender, who wanted to revolutionise the revolution, had left, aware of the irreconcilable breach between them, and this partly freed the way. But there were other impediments, men who believed they had the right to their own opinions, and who were growing more and more arrogant by the day. This was not how Fidel had envisaged it would be.

Then, as always happens with true leaders, unlike timid souls who give in out of fear of consequences, El Comandante made a decision. Someone would have to be severely punished to set an example for the rest. If one of the leaders of the rebellion were targeted, the others would understand, once and for all, who was in charge and what the revolution stood for.

Who would be chosen? Who would have the honour of being immolated for the supreme ideal? Who would be the sacrificial lamb?

Out of the various candidates whose curriculum Fidel

scrutinised to assess revolutionary importance and the extent to which their ideas diverged from his own, one stood out as having all conditions required for the sacrifice. He was insubordinate, headstrong, and determined, and, to make matters worse, he had an intense charisma that sometimes outshone Fidel's. He had challenged Fidel on more than one occasion, almost going as far as to threaten him. The people, particularly the peasants, venerated him, seeing him as their representative.

Camilo Ochoa's fate was sealed.[3]

Drug dealing, the apogee of capitalist decadence, would be the charge, supported by irrefutable evidence, both true and false. Men whom Fidel trusted, who had been threatened with death in case they weakened, would stage the circus necessary for the fall of the daring trapeze artist. And once he was flat on his back, bones smashed and vital organs crushed, there would be no medicine able to heal him. Some people would probably have doubts about Camilo Ochoa's guilt, while others would never agree to the charges laid against him. In other words, no one would believe it at all! But that didn't matter, if the point was to teach the conspirators a lesson. And there were no doubts that the lesson would be learned by all, and everyone would be convinced that, from then on, only one man could dare fly without a safety net.

Camilo Ochoa was arrested in the early hours of the morning in his house, where policemen found undeniable proof of his guilt, a bag of cocaine, and he was carried off to a clandestine prison. Newspapers, radio, and television announced that one of the heroes of the revolution had, after all, been proved a traitor, having allowed himself to be corrupted by capitalist vices. Some journalists even rummaged through Camilo's past and produced a list of misdemeanors considered suspicious auguries of things to come. (He had, for example, once stolen a papaya in primary school, as his

---

3. see note at the end of the book.

teacher, a devoted and respectable elder of the revolution, clearly recalled.) His image was broadcast around the island, and grave words were spoken by circumspect commentators.

The bag of cocaine, which in fact was nothing more than flour and did not even belong to the supposed dealer, traveled the length and breadth of the island without ever leaving the safe into which it had been tossed as irrefutable proof, acquiring a legendary status never before granted to either drug or grain. Indeed, the island was intensely focused on the bag, which everyone knew was not Camilo Ochoa's (although no one knew what it actually contained). Once the official version (said to be true) had been launched, other versions (said to be false) multiplied; but as the first was false and those that opposed it were closer to the truth, truth and falsehood changed places, with each in the domain of the other. This might have seemed confusing, but in reality, no one had any doubts as to which was which.

Contrary to what was claimed, this time no one rejoiced in the fall of a just man. The disgrace of the hero, whose virtues often served as a foil to random mediocrity, a polished mirror that uncovered deformed faces and multiplied warts, did not bring any joy to the people.

As might be expected, there were no doubts. Camilo Ochoa confessed to the crime at the trial, broadcast on television. As sentences were generally executed before the judge's decision, provided they were not the death sentence, the defendant realised he was condemned from the moment of his arrest. Thus, Camilo Ochoa knew there was no point trying to protest his innocence, or refute the incriminating witnesses – should there perchance have been any manipulation of the evidence. As this was an irreversible process completely out of his control, a whirlpool already sucking him down to unknown depths, the only thing left to him was to make sure no one else was dragged down with him.

Thus, as no baker had been called to bear witness, he remained impassive as other genuine drug dealers identified him as the kingpin of the illegal narcotics trade, and he showed no reaction when relatives and childhood friends expressed their indignation at his attempts to lure them into the criminal ring that he masterminded. Only when his accuser alleged that he had become a revolutionary to better develop his despicable activities did Ochoa manage a weak smile. 'I confess,' were the only words he spoke when the torrent of accusations – the rumble of thunder that precedes the deadly lightning strike – finally ceased.

The defence lawyer, in the few opportunities he was given to speak, discoursed on the advanced nature of the law that governed the island, insisting that no one was above it, and, imperturbable, demanded justice. In that sombre masked ball, where each vibrating note heralded infinite possibilities of death, the participants composed their features accordingly: the prosecutor and judges adopted an expression of disgust and indignation to hide the shame in their eyes; the counsel for the defence wore an air of moral authority and wisdom to camouflage the pathos in his eyes; and Camilo Ochoa chose an expressionless mask that annulled all emotion. And so, as anticipated, justice was done.

One day, Camilo Ochoa, condemned to life imprisonment and exhausted with the loneliness of a solitary cell that excluded the sun, decided to escape to where no one could ever catch him.

Having fallen through the trapdoor into a dream (in this case a nightmare), Fidel began to hear irate voices. He gradually became aware of a hysterical crowd emerging from a mist and threatening him. Although he could not see his own body, he felt it present in the dreamscape, knowing it to be the target of the clamouring mob. No one would come to protect him; the enraged multitude was his own people. The demonstrators' shouts grew louder and louder as they drew closer, their faces distorted in murderous fury. Armed with sticks and farming implements, they razed everything that stood in their path, knocking down his revolution as if it were a house of cards. Commanding them, his fist clenched in the air, was Camilo Ochoa.

Then the telephone rang. With a start, Fidel opened his eyes and mechanically stretched out his arm for the receiver. An agitated voice said: 'El Comandante, there's rioting in the streets.'

'Get the leader! Arrest him!'

'I'm sorry, Comandante, but we don't know who is leading the rabble.'

Until that point, Fidel had been absolutely convinced of what he was saying, but suddenly he was plunged into a state of confusion that left him dumb, suspended in a web somewhere between illusion and reality. He wanted to say, 'Idiots, I've just seen him,' but he waited a few seconds before breaking free of the trap he'd entangled himself in. 'Tell me calmly what's going on.'

Soon he was again inside the car that had brought him less than an hour before, repeating the same journey in the opposite direction, this time so fast he scarcely glimpsed the last moments of the dramatic combat between the static sugarcane and frantic cutters. Fidel wondered what attitude he should take before his people, who were now apparently booing and hissing him. As the impossible had occurred, he had to rise to the occasion, whatever happened. The slightest hesitation in his voice, a wrong word, an insecure glance would be enough to cause the rabble to attack like frenzied animals, sensing weakness in their prey.

Fidel had already defied firearms, the loneliness of imprisonment, and threats from the most powerful countries on earth, but this was the first time he had had to confront his own people, those who had so often applauded him and sworn their eternal devotion. However, like all predestined beings, he enjoyed an important advantage. The wolves that were now gnashing their teeth, getting ready to tear him apart, had till recently been gentle lambs willing to do his every bidding. Thus, Fidel sensed hidden weaknesses in his opponents' strength.

Moments before, the insurgents had been shouting 'Freedom!' and 'Down with tyranny!' but they now fell silent. The clamour of the crowd, charged with a powerful energy that seemed to multiply tenfold when each new man joined his voice to the others, began to subside the moment the protesters glimpsed the black car heading toward them. It was extinguished completely when the dreaded passenger erupted from it.

Silence fell.

The sun, burning from the friction of the heavens, gradually lowered toward the sea. A shaft of light fell across Fidel's back, illuminating the faces of his opponents. But while he experienced this as an almost pleasurable caress, a dazzling beam blinded the crowd. And so it was that quite distinct and opposite reactions were produced in the two parties that now faced each other head-on, as if some mysterious cosmic force were regulating the island's destiny. Fidel, enjoying being stroked by the warmth, felt strength flowing into his muscles, radiating vigour and determination. The people, trying to shade their eyes from the blinding light, were overcome with an intense fatigue, which dampened their convictions, leaving them disoriented and confused.

El Comandante was now a fearsome matador, and indeed, many tails and ears had been cut off in the past from bleeding impotent bulls. Or perhaps El Comandante was the beast, powerful and indomitable, preparing to charge on a handful of second-rate bullfighters, weak and fearful. The sunny arena had become a prohibited space, an unknown frontier, which, once crossed, could bring either disgrace or glory.

Intense silence pressed on the eardrums of everyone present, as if there had been a sudden change of pressure when the clamour ceased. In the presence of El Comandante, the distinction between policemen and demonstrators blurred, and they all became a band of men and women awaiting a terrible punishment. The divinity had descended to Earth and had come to settle accounts with the worshippers of the golden calf that had disobeyed him. Leaning against each other, trying to derive strength from the weakness of the rest, they were united by anguish at the imminent verdict; the forces of law and order felt guilty for not having prevented the demonstration, and the people felt guilty for having demonstrated. The only audible sound was breathing, which they all tried hard to stifle so as not to be noticed. Fidel conducted this silent orchestra, which operated in perfect time, producing music to his taste. No variations in rhythm or alterations in pitch disturbed its monotonous repertoire.

Suddenly, without lowering the baton held pointed at their heads, he decided to interrupt the concert to converse with the musicians. 'What's going on? Why are you protesting?'

With these words, El Comandante, genuinely perplexed, embarked on an improvised speech. No one dared reply to his questions, so he continued, insisting that the country was undergoing a very serious crisis due to enemy sabotage, that the claw of capitalism was trying to asphyxiate the economy, and that hard times were in store for all citizens. Having diagnosed their present problems and predicted even worse for the future, he then appealed to their collective resistance and revolutionary spirit, recalling the heroic struggles that had led them to triumph over the exploiters of the people, and the progress and conquests made through the revolution. Finally, he reminded them that the end of all this would mean a return to slavery, and he promised the crisis would be overcome and they would all be rewarded for their patriotic efforts.

The deathblow had been given. The bull had tossed away the *toreadors*. However, Fidel was not yet satisfied. He had repeated the same arguments time and time again, until they had become a tasteless mass that he thrust down the throats of his glutted company. They, with mouths open, partook endlessly of the revolutionary host offered by the high priest despite waves of nausea. Then, before the first symptoms of indigestion set in, the demonstrators responded in chorus to

Fidel's prompts with clenched fists raised in the air. 'Long live Fidel.' 'Long live the Revolution.' 'Long live El Comandante.' It was as if they had received a stimulus that compelled them against their wills, forcing them to behave in a way odious to them. Their bodies obeyed an absurd order, ignoring the desire to resist. And thus they remained in a hypnotic trance, just as convinced as when they were baying for his resignation. For long minutes, their erstwhile leaders were forced to prove their patriotic fervour to the point of ridicule, until Fidel, avenged by the act of collective contrition, ordered them home.

They obeyed, confused and ashamed, wanting to tear the veins out of their wrists with their teeth. On the way, their eyes downcast, some dared call out new insults against El Comandante, once more demanding his resignation, but this time their words did not mesh, and no one heard them. Instead, they exploded silently inside their heads, as was proved by the smoke-reddened eyes. Nor could anyone see the arms frenziedly punching the air in defiance, for, like invalids, they were dreaming they had recovered their lost faculties.

By then, the sun had already drowned in the water.

The next day, the *Granma* reported that agitators had been trying to stir up trouble amongst the people but had been unmasked by the citizens themselves, who immediately organised a giant demonstration in support of El Comandante and the revolution. The whole population of the city spontaneously lent their support, respectfully falling silent upon the arrival of Fidel, after which they went on to demonstrate their unconditional support for him. As proof, the first page showed a photograph of him being greeted by an enthusiastic crowd with fists clenched in the air. This incident, it was concluded, demonstrated two things: that the agitators would use all means to achieve their ends, but that the people's reaction showed once more that the fatherland had the capacity to defeat the enemies of the revolution. Taking these two facts into account, all citizens were advised to be particularly vigilant and to be prepared to act upon the slightest suspicion.

Having won the battle, Fidel felt rather lost. He suspected the war would be long and the only outcome would be defeat. The people considered him an enemy, along with JFK, and were prepared to fight him. In an attempt to understand these recent events and the complaints made against him, he tried to get beyond the standard reasoning processes used by the regime and avail himself of the enemy's logic.

Without needing to exchange his camouflage gear for a suit and tie, splash on eau de cologne, or buy a mobile phone, he thought himself into the mind of a democrat (for him, a depraved bourgeois capitalist). This empathetic experience was rather humiliating, but it provided him with precious information he could never have obtained through traditional methods. Those methods, El Comandante well knew, only led to soothing but false conclusions. His counsellors (if he still had any) would not have dared let the fuelless locomotive they were dragging behind them come off its ideological rails. Using this method he managed to glean some idea of the real motivations behind his citizens' discontent and assess the extent of his own responsibility. That is to say, only by distorting his vision of reality was he able to see with any clarity what was before his eyes.

Despite all this, Fidel remained absolutely sure of one thing. He might be defeated by others, yes, but he would never give in to himself!

That night, El Comandante encountered another challenge – a storm over his bed. The sheets became sweat-soaked waves, his pillow lost in the surf, and his own body was dragged from one side of the bed to the other by the squalls. This strange phenomenon lasted for hours, redoubling in intensity just as it seemed to be quietening, and then suddenly calming at the point of greatest turbulence. Finally, the forces of nature exhausted their ire and there came a lull, bringing with it sleep. At that point he disappeared into non-existence.

At midday, Fidel made his first attempt to return from

the only refuge he had managed to find, but his feeble efforts ended in sweet failures that prevented him from returning to reality. Cradled in the belly of sleep, he resisted the contractions of wakefulness, trying his best to avoid a traumatic birth. However, gestation time was up and, after unsealing his eyes, he found that he was being pushed out, limb by limb, into the hostile world he himself had created. When the process was over, he found himself completely alone and unprotected, with no one to pick him up and nurse him at their breast.

As silently as workers unloaded the cargo containers onto the quay, Varadero left the ship. A link of some sort had broken on the crossing, weakened, no doubt, by his and JFK's actions. Confused, like someone who feels pain yet cannot locate its source, Varadero fell quiet. He didn't really know what emotion to adopt. Like someone at a solemn ceremony who hesitates between joy and sadness and ends up confusing the two, he was cleft, and the opposing sides clashed together, leaving a single victim. There was nothing he could do about it. He had already lost control of the bumper cars lodged inside his head. The drivers were beside themselves. All he could do was wait until one of them ran out of fuel. But until that happened – and it might not since he owned the petrol station that refuelled both – the torture was tearing him apart.

His mission on behalf of Fidel had gone completely contrary to plan. He had obtained no important information and had more than once forgotten what he was supposed to be doing in enemy territory. His cover had been blown because he had become a regular presence at private parties, where guests were delighted with his mojitos. What is more, he had even gone swimming in the sea with his enemy, who had then set him free. It was straight out of a novel or film, something that could never happen in real life.

Back in his home city, as automatic pilot took him along routes engraved in his memory, he felt something was different, though everything was apparently the same. And the differences, tangible yet nonexistent, seemed to accentuate as he approached the places he used to frequent and recognised smells, saw familiar faces, and greeted acquaintances in the street. He wondered if he had, in fact, returned to his country, or if he had not disembarked on another island that was vaguely similar. Finally, when he realised all the reference points were still the same and that the problem must be in himself, he began to wonder who he was, after all, and what he should do.

These ruminations seemed to set in motion a huge complex mechanism, something like a windmill whose blades turned against the wind, and he found his strength being syphoned. He was dizzy and shivering, with twinges of pain. For a moment, it seemed as if his internal organs had become disconnected and, instead of functioning in synchrony to achieve an autonomous performance, were competing with each other.

Varadero had been trained to resist endless interrogations, sleep deprivation, and electric shocks, and was used to cheating hunger without food and food without hunger. In such situations, he would dig in his heels and refuse to bend, completely sure of his limitless psychological endurance. This, however, was something he had not been prepared for, an unknown game with hidden rules and inscrutable objectives.

He sat down.

Before him was an old ruined palace, which, like him, looked as if it was on the point of collapse. But the building had made a pact with time, while Varadero's structure was coming apart so fast that it seemed centuries of erosion had been condensed into an hour. Thus, despite the great differences separating stone from flesh, and insensible masonry from complex thought, both were under threat, in time frames impossible to predict. Renovation might have restored the palace to its former glory, but Varadero was too far gone. The only way he could be salvaged was for the old structure to be demolished and a new one built.

In the sky, the flock of celestial sheep gradually moved, chameleon-like, from orange pastures to purple ones and finally to grey.

Varadero sat there motionless, eyes absorbed, unaware of the pulsations of the city and the marvels of nature. Nightfall was announced by the luminous eyes of a car that took its attention off the road to observe the man sitting on the pavement. The indiscretion made him jump, and he raised his arms and hands instinctively to shield his eyes against the beam emitted by the pop-eyed orbits of the vehicle.

He gradually became aware of how much time had passed since his strength had failed him, though he could not remember what he had thought about during this time. He thrust his fingers into his hair, tugging and twisting it like straw on a pitchfork, in the hope that such toil might bring some clarity to his thoughts.

He got up and walked on, directionless, impelled by mechanical impulses that forced him on rhythmically like a stubborn marionette. His will was no more than a muscular contraction that originated in the legs and spread to the rest of the body. But it was an iron will, for he felt a pressing need to walk as if that action had become an essential biological function, like breathing or the beating of his heart. In this way, he gradually found the right pace, adjusting it when he came to a slope, advancing without effort, unable to stop himself. He didn't even feel the increase in his body temperature or the first warnings of the torn skin on his toes. To stop now would be to thwart the natural impetus of his body, propelled as it was by the energy of imprisoned winds. As he walked, he no longer saw or heard, for his mind was occupied with more important issues than the reality of the city, and the hubbub of his inner voices stifled the noises of the night. Nevertheless, he managed to avoid obstacles through sheer instinct.

Inside a bubble, he floated aimlessly on the breeze.

God and Christ were surely observing him, perhaps even monitoring his progress, having reserved some crucial role for him in the future. For Varadero managed to proceed unscathed, though he wandered along so erratically that anyone else would soon have been brought to a tragic end. He found impossible spaces in the middle of a compact platoon of bicycles, anticipated a crossing so precisely that only his back was grazed by passing trucks, and always took the right decision at traffic lights on great avenues full of furious vehicles.

But, after hours of wandering back and forth, repeating trajectories and confronting dangers already defeated, his spy brain – that gas-filled balloon – reached maximum dilation point. Varadero let forth a primal shriek that rebounded in the distance, causing shivers to ripple through the darkness. His clenched fists opened like a bow next to his chest, and arrows of sound propelled from his lungs.

Police officers, security guards, and curious members of the public trailed wearily to the scene and found themselves confronted with a figure heaped on the pavement. 'Only a drunkard,' they decided, relieved that no political motives were underlying this disturbance of public peace. A small crowd gathered, watching Varadero attentively. Some of them grabbed his feet and shook him to confirm the diagnosis that had been proffered. Relieved that the infected waters of the regime had not been stirred up, they hauled him to his feet, censuring such anti-revolutionary behaviour. 'Shame on you, comrade,' they said, even though some of them really were drunk.

The spontaneous gathering soon broke up as interest dissipated and curiosity gave way to boredom. Held up by some, pushed by others, and feeling less tense but still confused, Varadero went on his wandering way, this time followed by a pack of stray dogs. For various reasons, the canines had also responded to his howl, perceiving that a human was desperately in need of help. From a dog's perspective, a man can be both a god to be worshipped or a fragile creature in need of protection, and in either case he is prepared to serve him for the rest of his life. Seeing him prostrate, they licked his face and tugged at his clothing, trying to revive him. They growled protectively whenever humans drew near. Unable to understand Varadero's internal conflict, they sensed his fragility and escorted him silently. They would have put him out of his misery, had it been necessary, but for now they were prepared to give their own lives to defend him. The passers-by could not get near him for he was surrounded by an implacable bodyguard, ready to attack; thus, a way opened up before him on the pavement.

The spy's security corps, which contained dogs of all sizes, types, and colours, could have been taken as a model of a just society in which everyone was given equal opportunity. Or, it could have served as an example of a dictatorship in which the tyrant needs a praetorian guard just to venture out into the street. For Varadero it was much simpler. Accompanied by animals, feeling their soft fur and hot breath on his hands, he recovered his inner peace.

Strategically placed cannons relentlessly bombarded the target, emitting powerful blasts of sounds. Different coloured spotlights alternated explosions of light with sudden eclipses. Their targets, trying in vain to escape, jerked about rapidly, making strange feints in which feminine dexterity had the edge over male inertia. Eyes met and swerved away, generating a tangle of perspectives that varied with the observer's angle and individual perception, like a Cubist painting. Sudden clouds of smoke enveloped the scene. To compensate for high temperatures, or perhaps to raise them even more, those who had not ventured into the bombardment zone tipped diverse alcoholic beverages down their throats.

Lost on the dance floor, right foot constantly struggling against the left, Varadero seemed to be waging war with the music. His eyes were closed, and he felt himself alone, not in the disco but elsewhere, though this sensation was belied by the fact that he was constantly getting elbowed in the ribs and trodden on by the other dancers. Nearby, a well-dressed, middle-aged woman (who was, in fact, Fidel Castro in disguise) was shaking herself frenetically, spreading the aroma of expensive perfume. Attracted by the scent, Varadero's attention returned to the dance floor, and he tried to make approaches to that beautiful creature who was sensually swaying her voluptuous body. He was aroused by this unexpected carnal vision. Feeling a new strength flowing into him and inflamed with lust, he suddenly began to leap around with arms outstretched. Fidel, taken aback, ignored these displays so typical of the excited male, without realising that this was his perfect spy.

El Comandante could only make out vague shadowy figures due to the refraction caused by his mirrored glasses, which he wore to ensure anonymity. There were two reasons for this artifice. One was that he wanted to assess the impact of capitalist entertainments upon the revolution. The other was that he also wanted to enjoy them himself without giving his enemies reasons to scoff.

Varadero was now dancing alongside Fidel, wondering how best he could approach this beautiful woman. El Comandante resisted this blatant harassment as best he could, taking care not to reveal his disguise. Suddenly, there erupted the rumble of a salsa mixed with electronic rhythms, provoking a collective frenzy, as the dance floor was taken over by eager dancers. Consisting of felines and pachyderms in roughly equal measure, they squealed with delight, becoming entwined in complex dances in which the concatenation of two opposing forces transformed the four-legged tangle into a sensual writhe.

Increasingly excited by the beautiful lady wriggling away from him and by the music pounding in his ears, Varadero grabbed Fidel around the waist and led him in a crazy dance that gradually swept everyone else off the dance floor. Soon they were the only pair left – an unexpected dance-floor revolution. Totally beside himself and whirling as if possessed, the spy flung Fidel about, pulled him, pushed him, twisted him, bent him over backwards, and lifted him to heights that sometimes defied the laws of gravity. Aware that he would suffer an even greater indignity if his true identity were exposed, El Comandante tried hard to keep up, shaking his shoulders and hips as best he could. And then, during a series of movements executed at breakneck speed, Varadero thrust Fidel on top of an amplifier and then jumped up to join him.

They then began squirming like lunatics, shaking their heads dementedly, while the other dancers rather apprehensively kept their distance. Sweaty and tousled, with shirt tails hanging out, Varadero began to shout disconnected phrases in English, and was imitated by Fidel, who yelled only 'Fight!' with his fist clenched. These cries were interpreted by the astonished DJ – who was still on a learning curve when it came to capitalist fetishes – as a request to up the volume of the music. The dancers poured back onto the dance floor, where they looked up at Varadero and Fidel as if in adoration of unknown pagan gods.

Accustomed to being worshipped by thousands of devout fans, El Comandante made a mental note to add electronic sounds to his six-hour rallies. Varadero, the main divinity in this bizarre ritual, continued to keep his eye on the magnificent woman who had bravely accompanied him through the dance display. He was completely oblivious to political concerns.

On the contrary, his mind was growing murky with perverse cogitations that were causing him to regress to a state of pure bestiality. Hostage to lust, in a prelude to a localised blood flux, he mentally undressed the magnificent body of his dancing companion, made more sensual by the fireworks of the psychedelic lighting. Fidel felt himself being stripped of his clothing piece by piece, and although this was only occurring in the depraved mind of Varadero, it nevertheless caused him great discomfort, probably due to some feminine sixth sense.

Finally, having stripped his victim completely naked – though his mental representation somewhat exceeded the damsel's true attributes, particularly in the area of the breasts and buttocks – Varadero surreptitiously pinched Fidel's backside, murmuring words in his ear that no one could hear but everyone could guess. Fidel felt an adrenaline rush, for this was clearly no invitation to take tea. With a feline leap, he hopped neatly over the dancers and landed on the bar, knocking over a Cuba Libre. Then he fled in disarray to the exit and was never seen again.

Disconsolate, Varadero struggled down from his improvised dance floor, paid his bill with false money, and under the sympathetic gaze of a group of thwarted Latin machos, left the discotheque downcast. Outside he discovered that the waiting dogs were snuffling a pair of pink high heels.

The next day, feeling even more confused, Varadero decided to present himself before Fidel to tell him the truth about his espionage mission. He decided to wear his secret agent outfit – a black suit, shirt, and shoes – despite the fact that it felt like a dead skin. Looking at himself in the mirror, he felt badly dressed and unsophisticated, without a drop of class.

That sense of discomfiture about his clothes was most certainly the result of the influences he had absorbed during his time in enemy lands. It was pernicious or positive, depending on one's political or moral perspective. For in that consumer society, to strut about in a fashionable bar in clothes from last year's collection, was, for all people of good taste, shameful, decidedly cheesy, and character defining. Nevertheless, it was thus attired – ridiculous for tropical climes, in mourning for certain Western cultures, and immediately recognisable to all passers-by – that the perfect spy headed toward the place where Fidel had told him he would be hiding.

Inside there was a devil on the loose; A powerful, irresistible devil urging him to do something dazzlingly reckless – to cross an irreversible boundary.

Fidel had chosen a white marble colonial-style mansion that was discreet, as it had only two columns at the entrance to support the entablature over the terrace and was smaller in size and less exuberantly decorated than other buildings along the avenue.

Fidel's transdisciplinary skill, which he had mastered better than anyone, enabled him to find the right balance among the needs for security, comfort, and revolutionary principles. He would never allow himself to fall into excess like some African dictator. Naturally, he was not going to hide away in one of those bug-ridden shacks that had started to spring up all over the island for lack of building materials. But neither was he going to succumb so easily to the temptations of capitalism by building a sumptuous oriental-style palace with gold taps and lifts. Modest mansions and country houses that had once belonged to Latino or Anglo-Saxon colonisers did the job perfectly, once they had been disinfested of cockroaches. And clearly it was Fidel's natural right – not an irony of destiny or confirmation of Marx's maxim about the repetitions of history and the role of farce – that he should occupy the homes of those who had previously been lords of the island.

This Marx had only come into the world to annoy everyone, not only the capitalists but everyone else too. Given time, veiled criticisms of the workers, too, would surely be found in his works. The man was intractable: all got up with that beard to make him look like a Bible prophet. You had to know how to use him. Things that were true over a century ago might not mean anything today.

Varadero arrived, perspiring and uncomfortable, unable to take in the details of the fine architecture or reflect on the logical complex of options underlying El Comandante's choice of hideaway. He combed his hair, using sweat to make the parting, which forced certain hairs to turn right and others to align with the left. Then, with his capillary ideology reestablished, he rang the bell.

Ding-dong. The door opened, and a moustached, square-faced guard growled, 'What do you want?'

'I've come to speak to El Comandante. I'm a secret agent.'

'There's no one here by that name,' replied the guard,

trying halfheartedly to hide the truth.

'Rubbish! I know very well that he's hiding here,' snapped Varadero, ready for anything.

'Who told you that?' replied the guard, who had been taught that one question should always be answered with another if he were to keep command of a situation.

'Fidel himself.'

Distrustful of the visitor's intentions, the guard launched into the spiel he used to deter undesirables. 'El Comandante does not receive visitors. All matters should be put in writing and addressed to the ministry—'

At this point, Varadero took from his pocket a Statue of Liberty miniature and showed it to the guard, who jumped, startled. 'Er, come in,' he stammered, as if burned by the torch.

Varadero was then led into a large hall decorated with black-and-white photographs of all the heroes of the revolution. Alone before this gallery of men alongside whom he had fought, planned operations, and carried out exceptionally risky missions, he felt ashamed, as if each face could discern the terrible inner conflict wracking him. It was as if they perceived his lack of faith and were profoundly disappointed at his betrayal. He stooped under the weight of the guilt, feeling unworthy to stand before them.

Then he began to tell them what he was feeling, in a sudden urge for catharsis, as if they could hear, give advice, or absolve him. He confessed to his doubts about the revolution, his fascination at discovering capitalism, and the new doubts growing in him. He expressed his remorse and shame, and he admitted that he felt completely bewildered. In his own defence, he also told those paper judges about his working in factories and fields, the numerous services he had provided to the fatherland, and the risks he had taken in his life. And as he listed his long revolutionary curriculum, he found himself revisiting those past events of which he had been so proud. Varadero was once again becoming the young idealist, ready to die for a different world, and knowing that if given the chance again he would follow any one of those figures to the ends of the earth, dispatching to heaven or hell those who got in their way.

Thus the past became the present, and recent events were buried in the depths of his memory, on which everything seemed to depend. At that moment, Varadero's memories were all linked together on an invisible chain, which brought them boiling to the surface, pearls randomly threaded on the necklace of a life.

Then, armed with his old machine gun, he fired rounds of bullets at the enemy forces that were trying to hide in the corners of the room, and dived under the carpet to escape a marksman entrenched behind a closet, lobbing grenades into his hideout.

'To remember is to live again,' said Fidel as he opened the door, even before he had laid his eyes on the perfect spy. He was well aware of the effect that this gallery of icons had on his visitors. For Varadero, whose back was turned to the door, Fidel's voice preceded his physical appearance, though he found he was able to visualise him with a clarity that could never have been achieved by his eyes alone. Then the opposite happened when he turned to face him, for in a near-catatonic state, Varadero found he couldn't hear anything that was being said at first. 'I'm happy to see you... you'll have a great many things to tell me, I suppose. What made you linger so long in the enemy's lands?' They both remained silent, the one because he hadn't actually heard any sound, the other waiting for one. A flying cockroach might have broken the silence if it had hit the light, exploded in midflight, or broken out into screams, but El Comandante used excellent insecticides.

'I prepared myself for that mission like never before. I studied the history of JFK's nation over and over again, its language and accent, the style of clothes they wear. That made it easy to infiltrate the people, imitate their habits, make friends, and tell the stupid jokes that they seem to appreciate so much. In fact, I became an exemplary capitalist citizen, to the point of internalising my own disguise. From the second month, I began to discover I did not dislike my new identity. At first, I tried to deny it, forcing myself to exaggerate the defects I found by counteracting them with the virtues of our regime. But little by little, as I tasted the previously unknown flavours of bourgeois comfort, my trick became ineffective till it eventually stopped working completely. There was nothing left for me other than to take refuge in the preparation of my spy reports, in the hope that the work would restore me to my right mind. But then I realised that I was shamefully praising capitalist society. From then on, everything got very confused. Or became very clear, I'm not sure which. Though I never stopped believing in the Revolution, I also understood what freedom truly meant. And to make things worse, I couldn't treat JFK as an enemy. But, do you know what the worst thing was about all this? What really bothers and perturbs me? I'm never going to be able to believe in you again, Comandante!'

These were the words that Varadero would have liked to utter to Fidel Castro. They came very close to reflecting his feelings, which were still new and strange to him, like a freshly learned language. Even so, despite not actually having hurled out that confession against Fidel, the simple fact of having produced it so courageously in his imagination gave him intense satisfaction.

'I prepared myself for that mission like never before. I studied the history of JFK's nation over and over again, its language and accent, the style of clothes they wear. That made it easy to infiltrate the people, imitate their habits, make friends, and tell the stupid jokes they seem to appreciate so much. In fact, I became an exemplary capitalist citizen, to the point of internalising my own disguise. Now I truly understand the meaning of capitalist alienation, the compulsive consumption of material goods, the unbridled competition between people. I was able to obtain precious information about our enemies. The child labour, the exploitation of immigrants, the drugs, and prostitution. All of it is true! I have also got proof that they have powerful armies and are obsessed with destroying us. But then I was taken prisoner and subjected to endless interrogations and the most inhumane treatment. Still, they didn't get anything out of me, not a peep. In frustration, they tried to buy me off, offering me political asylum. My response was to escape. I have returned from hell, Comandante, and I am at your disposal!'

These were the words that Varadero actually uttered, using ready-made phrases he had heard time and time again throughout his life, many from Fidel himself. He was convinced this version would please El Comandante. He spoke in a firm voice and looked Fidel in the eye. Fidel, for his part, merely listened in silence, and then stepped forward and embraced the perfect spy with vigour. 'The fatherland will not forget your sacrifices, comrade!'

Fidel had almost no doubts that Varadero would continue to be faithful. Nevertheless, that same day, he ordered his arrest.

As he often did when overcome with anxiety, El Comandante resorted to an imaginative disguise. This time he went out into the street dressed as a blind man in search of the only human beings who could console him in his moments of affliction, which were becoming ever more frequent. With his hat, green-lensed glasses, and metal cane, he made his way nimbly up the avenues, side roads, and alleys, exceeding the speed limit advisable for his fictitious character. He was prompted by his refined sense of smell, searching out the acrid odours of misery. That day, like any other, it was not difficult to encounter men, women, and, above all, children who desperately needed to recover their hope in the revolution.

The first marvellous encounter occurred when he spied an old man with one leg struggling hard to move forward a few centimetres. The second was a woman disfigured with the abstract lines of facial scars. Finally, he came face-to-face with a little blind girl, tapping the ground with her crude cane and reaching out to touch the void in front of her. He observed everything carefully, taking in all the details of the disabilities and deformities that presented themselves before him. Before the amputee, he breathed a sigh of relief for having two legs that could raise him before his people and his enemies. Before the disfigured woman, he took joy from the fact that his past battles had not left any marks that could diminish his charisma. And watching the little blind girl, he understood how fortunate he was to be able to look at the world, even if he only saw misery. Then, having deluded his pain and rediscovered his hope, he returned home calmer, with a new, almost radiant, appearance.

The chicken's beady eye stared at the man who was getting ready to cut off its head. Chickens may be stupid, but they are incredibly brave. Unless, of course, it is their stupidity that dulls their sense of danger and gives them that air of confidence. But if an intense belligerent stare is a sign of courage for human beings and some other mammals, why shouldn't it be for poultry as well? Only because their brains are no bigger than their eyes?

In fact, we are all equal, though some of us are more equal than others, which shows that men are close to pigs and that chickens will always be poultry. In any case, how else should a black chicken behold an old man with a white beard wielding a sharpened knife? If it deflected its gaze, they would say that it was not only stupid but also unconscious. If its eyes showed any fear, it would be called chicken. If it looked supercilious, it would be considered an idiot or a snob. As such, the best attitude for a chicken to adopt when someone is preparing to sever its head from its neck – whether it is to be plucked, to be used for giblet rice, or in a Santería ritual[4] – is to maintain a fixed gaze, even if doing so reflects an almost total lack of neurons, and to ignore unfounded criticisms, whether they

---

4. Practiced originally in Cuba, Santería is a syncretic religion of West African and Caribbean origin that merges the Yoruba religion with Roman Catholicism.

come from members of their own species, humans, or pigs. In any case, the outcome would be the same whatever attitude it chose to adopt: decapitation in a single blow.

As the dark blood spurted into a pot, the old santero began to call upon the syncretic divinities, a blend of Yoruba[5] and Catholic. He had placed some strings of blue and green beads around Fidel's neck and ordered him to sit in an old armchair that had broken springs. Then he signalled to his helpers to begin banging their drums. As the blood from the chicken ran hot and sticky and the ceremonial music grew louder, Fidel watched the santero make contact with the gods. Concentrating deeply, and wholly secure in his own power, he launched into a ritual dance that involved brusque convulsions and broad gestures. And in this electrified struggle, the priest recklessly shook off the years like dust, exposing a childish restlessness beneath his venerable age.

For a few moments, Fidel felt alone and abandoned, so involved were the santero and his disciples in the ceremony, which, unlike anything else that took place on the island, was completely outside his control. Watching those participants in this magic ritual (they were perhaps party members, or maybe sophisticated traitors), he came to the conclusion that no ideological power would ever be able to compete with religion. Indeed, in times gone by, he himself had once considered taking the cloth. When educated humans allowed themselves to be embroiled in the mists of magic, inspiring inebriating vapours of superstition and irrationality, then the limits of the revolution became clear. Though no limit existed when El Comandante himself partook of that same ritual.

At that moment, he was feeling a powerful impulse to get up and arrest everyone present, divinities included. However, he remained seated, unable to move, waiting for some miraculous

---

5. Yoruba is the indigenous religion of the Yoruba-speaking people in Yorubaland, the region made up of southwestern Nigeria and parts of Benin and Togo.

revelation to solve the problems that he knew were unsolvable. His body was fused to the chair under its own weight, inviting him to a resigned inaction. And so he fell inert, slipping into a torpor of the kind that the python experiences as it digests its meal.

However, the dictator's almost imperceptible voice did not go unheard by the supernatural beings that had been summoned by the santero, for they had ultrasensitive eardrums and narcissistic temperaments. Ogum, the lord of war for some, bronzed St. Anthony[6] for others, detected the wisp reverberations coming from the El Comandante and did not much appreciate what he heard. So, partly due to the invocations that were in progress, partly due to the temptations offered by Fidel, and partly because he was getting bored, Ogum wasted no time in descending to Earth in a titanic fury.

Though Fidel Castro had only participated in one revolution against a puppet dictator, contained an invasion by mercenaries, and participated in an attempt to destroy the world, this self-important little man thought himself a great warrior. He hadn't even been in a real war! So Ogum, determined to teach Castro a lesson, decided to enter his body, take over his soul, and then leave him in shreds, completely devoid of all will. After all, other bold warriors who considered themselves daring and skilful enough to challenge him had been reduced to the consistency of a boiled vegetable for much less. And now this stubborn, bearded character, descendant of Galicians, had come to affront him without so much as a by-your-leave! These days, not even the gods are respected. Some unforgettable corrective remedy most certainly had to be applied.

Thus began Ogum's epiphany.

His appearance was accompanied by strange phenomena. Red lights erupted over Fidel's head, straightening out his

---

6. Ogum, a Yoruban deity, is often identified with Saint George as well as Saint Sebastian and Saint Anthony.

crinkled hair. Then the rumble of thunder caused those same hairs to stand on end. Finally, a great torrent of rain soaked the hair through. As Ogum was the patron of warriors, and not a hairdresser trainee, the successive transformations to the commandant's coiffure, which touched upon various styles and fashions might have signalled something meaningful, a hidden intention that needed to be deciphered, like Samson and Delilah, for fans of biblical parallelisms. However, it did not mean anything because the gods love confusing their believers and leaving behind unsolvable mysteries just to test their followers' faith. And, of course, a being from beyond cannot appear just like that, as if he were a mere beggar. A little pomp and circumstance never went amiss, and indeed is necessary to mark out differences, whether these differences lie between gods and men, nobles and plebeians, or tyrants and their subjects.

With his ethereal mass, Ogum prepared to break into Fidel's body and savagely take possession of him. Thus, like an Olympic athlete about to plunge from a high diving board he focused on his target, flexed his knees, and fearlessly launched himself headfirst at Fidel's skull. Under normal conditions, the god of war would have slid smoothly into the crystalline waters of his victim's brain, crushing it and taking possession of his soul. But these were not normal conditions.

The collision between the two skulls was brutal. Tectonic. On Ogum's side, the crash could be heard hundreds of kilometres away, causing the other divinities to rush to the site of the impact. There they beheld a scene never before witnessed: Ogum prostrate on the ground with a great bruise on his forehead. On Fidel's side, things appeared differently: there was a slight cracking sound, which got lost among the drumbeats. *Crack!* Fidel scratched his nape and had the strange presentiment that he was being watched.

Rather taken aback, the santero hung a sign on the door reading, 'Closed for stock taking'. Ogum, feeling a little fragile, discreetly withdrew and never messed with Fidel Castro again. As for El Comandante, he resignedly began to prepare to launch the mother of all invasions.

All these events were witnessed by God and Christ. God was concerned because he didn't have the faintest idea how to avoid the forthcoming tragedy. Christ was even more worried, because he knew he was usually assigned to the most serious cases and sent on impossible missions. From their celestial box on high, father and son had watched the development of the conflict between JFK and Fidel Castro – an ancient, intractable dispute – with growing interest, resisting the temptation to catch a glimpse of what was going on in other worlds.

God was of the opinion that the time had come to intervene. Christ disagreed. For the Creator, the growing internal opposition to Fidel's regime had brought to an end the commandant's illusions that the revolution would continue throughout his lifetime and perhaps even after his death. His illusions were compelling him to desperate acts (Varadero's imprisonment was undeniable proof of this), the climax of which would certainly be a suicidal attack on the nation of JFK. Christ agreed with these premises but believed that conditions were not yet ripe for a divine intervention that would change the history of humanity once and for all.

However, the conversation about the Castro-JFK war revived some divine phantoms that were repressed in the subconscious of the Creator; he too was subject to doubt from time to time, demonstrating just how complex and ephemeral was the understanding between parents and their children.

'If we don't do anything, something terrible will happen. Or even worse, they'll say it was our fault.'

'Don't upset yourself. Just as they've stripped us of our merits, so they'll exempt us from responsibilities. You'll see. Just as they invent theories to explain the beauty of a flower, so they will find a way of justifying killing between men.'

'Fine words, but one day someone will use mathematical

formulas and computer programs to prove we don't exist—'

'First of all, there are a great many people that no longer believe. Second, that would mean that our problems would be over.'

'And then what would we do? What sense does it make for us to be considered products of the human imagination?'

'Aren't you the one that usually has an answer for everything?'

This was followed by some moments of somewhat embarrassing divine silence. Then, after millennia of celestial contention, God decided to bare his soul.

'I confess I'm intrigued. Could there be someone above us? Who created me, then?'

'No one. You are the only being that has not been created.'

'But that is completely illogical, an affront to basic rationality.'

'What is fascinating in this mystery of origins and beginnings is that not even we understand it.'

Absorbed in the contemplation of the firmament, God digressed. 'To have no beginning and no end…'

'The specialist books on the subject insist that we are immortal…'

'Would that be a gift or a punishment?' Christ looked confused but God went on with his musings. 'I also wanted to have a father and a mother.'

'You have billions of children.'

'I sometimes wonder if their real father wasn't someone else.'

'It's the adoptive father that counts.'

'But, if I created them in my own image, then why do they behave as they do?'

'You're in no position to complain. Before I was born, you were terribly mischievous. And in any case, you gave them freedom of choice, free will.'

'That doesn't seem to have been a very good idea.'

'That's the problem. Only thinking beings can conceive

transcendental existence. Can you imagine a turkey in a mystic ecstasy, contemplating his magnificent baroque sculptures?' God frowned. He'd never been very keen on sacred art.

'We're getting off the subject.'

'It's all related, can't you see? Your creation is trying to break free of its creator. Look, they have already discovered that you didn't mould them out of clay and that women were not made from a man's rib. Nowadays almost everyone agrees they're descended from apes. No one believes in Hell; no one goes to confession. They've even managed to create test-tube babies and clones.'

'Are you telling me I've been fired?'

'You can't be fired because you're the boss. What they want is to set up on their own.'

'But why are they so rebellious?'

Christ hesitated before replying, and his countenance grew serious.

'I suspect that none of them, not even those that claim to be believers, are really convinced that another life exists.'

God placed his hand on his forehead and closed his eyes. 'So, what do they believe in, then?'

'Oh, they believe in power and money, in the good life, wild parties, things like that.'

God was temporarily lost in eschatological ruminations. 'You know, son, maybe you're right. I sent you to Earth to save men, but they ended up fighting amongst themselves in your name, enslaving each other and burning people on bonfires.'

'Even the angels defy you. What do you expect?'

'I might be old, but I'm not finished yet. I can still conjure up a plague or two.' God began to sing an old song. 'Look at me, I am old, but I'm happy…'

Christ countered, 'From the moment I could talk, I was ordered to listen…' Their exchange continued.

'Plagues? They would invent a cure right away and say it was all caused by genetic mutations.'

'You're right, the time for anger and revenge is over. This

time, we're going to think before we act.'

'I warn you, father, I'm not going to be the court jester all over again. With me, history doesn't repeat itself.'

'All right. But don't forget the great religious, philosophical, and political influence that you have over these two men. JFK doesn't lift a finger without invoking your name, and Fidel thinks he's applying the principles of equality that you preached. In their own muddled way, they're both trying to imitate you. In fact, if we look at the situation carefully, it wasn't really me that created them, it was you. They're your kids, son!'

Now although Christ was used to being accused of all kinds of things and to shouldering the blame for others, his mouth dropped open in stupefaction. 'So it's my fault now? Me? And I... not even with Magdalene.'

After this disconcerting dialogue, God retired into the clouds with an infernal headache. Now he had two problems to sort out. Christ remained where he was, paralysed by the unexpected dilemma that his father had thrust upon him yet unable to push away the chalice that was offered.

As these two reactions to adversity (movement and quiet) were quite different, even opposing, we might deduce that when the gods, like men, find themselves under pressure, just about anything could happen. Indeed, that might explain the frequent bouts of divine ire in the Old Testament, the slaughtered lambs, Christ's rage at the moneylenders, the cruel vengeance exacted by mythological gods, and Orisha's sudden fits of fury. In fact, only Buddha, who's not really a god at all, has managed to keep out of brawls when he finally managed to liberate himself from all desires except food!

III

FÁTIMA

From their hilltop vantage, JFK and the counsellor looked down on the excavations in progress, astounded by how the flat terrain was being transformed into a field of lunar craters. The pits ran in symmetrical rows, their teeth of sharpened stakes awaiting men and animals. 'Amazing. I've never seen anything like it, but do you really think all these holes will work?'

'Calm yourself, counsellor. These traps are highly effective. Half of Fidel's army will fall into them and the other half will run away, stricken with terror.'

Before the counsellor had the chance to remind the president that he should never underestimate his enemy, the lunchtime bugle made its strident call. Shovels and pickaxes dropped hastily in unison. Driven by an unstoppable energy called hunger, the workers rushed wildly up the hill. Their heavenly reward for digging hundreds of pits in a matter of hours awaited them at the top: a host of steaming cauldrons, bubbling with beans and bacon.

Confirming that cooking is one of the lynchpins of social division and justifying the revolutionary contempt for chefs, gourmet menus, and hors d'oeuvres, JFK, the generals, and the counsellor were served a different meal.

Sat well away from their vassals, on cushioned chairs at

a linen-covered table, grasping silver cutlery, they sampled an array of provisions – roast suckling pig, stewed capons, pan-roasted pheasant, and lamb hotpot served on the finest porcelain and washed down with red and white wines. Attentive and competent, the maître d' scuttled around the table. Notebook in hand, he probed guests in his subtle French accent. 'Is your meat well cooked, sir?' 'Would you prefer leg or breast?' 'I would recommend a Cabernet Sauvignon with this dish.'

Thus, with knives and forks, and more often than not with their bare hands, they bulldozed their way through the assortment of delicacies and quickly drained glasses of wine.

Given the importance of the event about to take place and the future of the nation resting on a knife's edge, a cavalcade of ideas on the matter were spewed around the table. 'What do those holes do actually?'

'I think the enemy is meant to fall into them.'

'What rot! They're for us to hide in.'

'This is an ecological disaster.'

For almost half an hour each defended his theory. Yelling, table thumping, and sighs of dismay were followed by food warfare. As if preparing for battle, some used olives and chicken legs as culinary ammunition to back the cause they were advocating.

Faced with such divergence of opinion, and such contrasting points of view, a particularly shrewd general, admired for his ability to unite rivals in a common cause, rose with difficulty from his chair. Emptying his glass of wine, he burped and said: 'My dear friends. Screw the holes, and the war! Let's get serious, now. Where are the whores?'

The question paralysed and silenced his audience. 'Oh hell, we forgot!' rung out the tragic chorus. A state of general consternation ensued, much greater than defeat in the war could ever have aroused. Heads bowed, grimacing with disappointment, they dejectedly pushed their plates to one side.

J. E. Hoover held his tongue, quietly leaving the table so that nobody would notice his absence. He felt like a stranger and had lost the will to counter their ideas. *It's just not worth it,* he told himself. Walking among the soldiers as they played cards, discussed football, or told jokes, he thought about how the only difference between them and the generals was position and power. Each behaved like the other, so long as a rise or fall altered the hierarchy.

There was a devil at loose within him, too.

'Dearest brethren, the antichrist has returned and is preparing to invade. The forces of evil march over our lands with nothing to stop them. The beast's hordes are unleashing their tentacles, thirsty for conquest. The dragon spews out the burning fire of hell. He comes to steal the fruits of our labour, enslave us, and assault our women. And why is this happening? Because you are unrepentant sinners. Because you don't give decent alms. Because you don't do what I tell you to do. Because you're a bunch of bastards and bitches. If it were up to you, the angels would lose their wings and get lice in their hair, the saints would repent their past lives, and even I would succumb to temptation. So this is your punishment, you mob: confront Fidel Castro and his armies. Let's get ourselves organised to stop that red devil from ruining our lives.'

From high in the pulpit, the priest evangelised vigorously about the Castro invasion, haranguing his flock about the fundamentals of religious practice, reminding them of their successive lapses, and justifying the approaching punishment. Strident and booming, his finger pointing to the sky or at his parishioners, waving his slipper threateningly at his terrified congregation, he reminded them of the irrefutable connection between sin and punishment, the consequence for disrespecting divine laws, shooting down bullets of morality, launching bombs of decency.

However, the learned priest and his flock did not realise that this punishment was quite different to the traditional ones. Here, they had the possibility of confronting it and of preparing some kind of resistance –though the chances of success were slight, unlike the old-fashioned sort that were sudden, violent, and unexpected.

Under the command of the priest, the population filled sandbags to form barricades. He chided them as they worked: 'Come on, you lazy good-for-nothings! Faster, faster!' The cleric had, in the meantime, exchanged his cassock for full fatigues, tied a black band around his head, and scratched one of his arms to give himself more credibility as a warrior. He was unable, however, to disguise the rolls of fat around his belly, to the disgust of the female parishioners and some of the men. From the steps of the pillory, the priest shrewdly oversaw the defensive operations while scribbling out schemes to resist the invader interspersed with drawings of naked girls.

The enemy attack had given him an authority he'd never dreamed of before, a power that seemed to have dropped from the sky. Thus, what appeared to everyone else as an ominous black threat was a rainbow of colourful opportunity for the priest, and he ardently wished that this situation of attack-not attack / kill-not kill would prolong indefinitely.

This change of mood brought a radical change to his sermons. 'My dearest brethren, the will of the Lord is inscrutable, so it is not worth trying to understand it. That is my job. And that is why I am telling you that Fidel's invasion is a true blessing for us all, the best thing that could have happened to our land, as we shall see. Before, you were all just snivelling black sheep, an undisciplined flock. No one cared about the other. Each of you was obsessed with your own success and with the wealth you wanted to make. Fraternity and compassion were forgotten. Now, though, faced with this hypothetical threat, you have discovered that by stretching out your hands to one another you can find a meaning for your pathetic existence. By putting aside your egoism, you have transformed this miserable village into a model of solidarity, charity, and forgiveness. You're still snivelling black sheep, that's for sure. But your hearts are in the right place. Let us pray, then, that the world be populated with Fidel Castros.'

Under the stony gaze of the malevolent beings imprisoned in the granite of the church walls, who were themselves intrigued by the sudden about-turn, this strange sermon reinforced the believers' conviction that thinking was something very complicated, only within reach of the elect, and that it was best not to blow their fuses. Resigned, they left the church with little will to reflect upon why some lambs were mystical while others were roasted in the oven with jacket potatoes.

The priest, for his part, doggedly studied Marxist economic theory at night, and pored over the authorised biographies of Fidel to make sure he would be ready for his enemy, should Fidel invite him to smoke some cigars. 'I am, after all, the only person in this god-forsaken place that can speak Latin.'

However, the priest, intoxicated by the inebriating vapours of absolute authority and convinced that no one would ever dare confront him again, had not counted on the appearance of the Revolutionary Movement of Patriotic Whores. It was thus, with amazement and incredulity, that he discovered, right in front of his own church, an awareness-raising session organised by the recently created RMPW.

Having decided to contribute their knowledge of human relations to the struggle against the invader, they had set up a movement to save the village from communism and limit the psychological suffering of its inhabitants. 'We don't want to be nationalised,' they said. 'The market is never wrong,' they claimed. After introducing their project, whose only concrete feature was the provision of a tent equipped with mattresses and mirrors for the emotional support of the brave defenders of the fatherland, they immediately launched an attack on the measures imposed by the priest. Atop a platform made of rotten planks, dressed in mini-skirts and high-heeled shoes, heavily made up, reeking of cheap perfume, and standing with hands on hips, they issued strident challenges in shrill voices, shaking their blonde highlights: 'What stupid strategy is this?' 'What qualifications does this gentleman have to decide what we should or should not do?' 'Who gave him the power to do that?' 'What are his real reasons, anyway?'

Bewildered by these inconvenient questions and not accustomed to challenging authority, the people glanced at one another distrustfully and murmured anxiously. Then, in the taverns, over beakers of wine, roast chorizo, hunks of corn bread, and olives, they heatedly discussed the RMPW's theories and the priest's role. In their homes, in the brief truce between outbreaks of quarrelling and mutual scoffing, husbands and wives finally found they had something to talk about. Even the priest, feeling harassed, was obliged to justify himself in his sermons, which he did wearing cassocks emblazoned with the colours of the national flag.

And so it was that, thanks to Fidel Castro, the society was divided into two irreconcilable factions, each as dogmatic and inflexible as the other, which, in the growing tension that preceded the outbreak of civil war, came to be known as the *Padristas* and *Putistas*[7].

For the *Padristas*, the padre was the only rightful leader of the resistance, the only person with the clear-sightedness needed. He was the richest man in the land and the most successful with the ladies, after all, and so it followed that he was the most able. The people had to obey him without questioning his orders. 'Believing, obeying, fighting' became their motto. Having once compared Fidel to a demon, the priest now seemed to recognise divine qualities in him. This was entirely natural, since in politics, today's truth is tomorrow's lies. Besides, the padre's defensive strategy was the only possibility.

For the *Putistas,* the padre was a fraud, and maybe even Castro's *Fifth Column*, making it vital to expose him and adopt other ways of fighting the enemy. Piling up sandbags was pointless as the Castro army had good ladders, and what's more it just wasn't right to waste good food on the

---

7. Whorists

enemy (hurling boiling lard!). And so, to avoid unnecessary massacre, they urged everyone to leave town immediately, set fire to it, and join the forces of JFK. However, in a kind of plan B, they did admit that if their plan was turned down, the best thing would be to welcome Fidel with open arms, calling him their liberator and denouncing the bourgeoisie in a cultural revolution never before seen.

Going beyond mere speech-making, political discussion, and putting up posters, the *Padristas* and *Putistas* organised street demonstrations aimed at winning over the citizens. The former set up a five-a-side football tournament, for which ten teams signed up. However, before a single game could be played, controversy struck when Putista teams accused the organisers of rigging the draw and refused to accept the referees chosen, as they believed them to be corrupt. This meant that the only games played were between Padrista teams. Even so, the same accusations of unfair refereeing were made and several pitch battles took place, resulting in a volley of broken legs and serious injuries. Faced with such a fiasco, the Putistas protested that the Padristas were incapable of organising anything, and that the doomed football tournament was a harbinger of bad things yet to befall the town.

The latter organised a beauty pageant, attracting nineteen young ladies, aged sixteen to twenty-five. Both traditional costume parade and the daring swimwear show went well. The general knowledge questions also went relatively well: 'Where is the Tower of Pisa?'

'Erm, in London?'

Even the girls seemed to share their most profound thoughts effortlessly: 'I wish for the good of humanity, world peace, I dunno, stuff like that.'

Then a *Padrista* contestant complained that the *Putista* contestants had breast implants, and all hell broke loose.

'These tits are natural.'

'Then let's squeeze them to see if they pop.'

'Girls, girls, please calm down.'

In the confusion that followed, with contestants refusing to undergo a manual and oral examination by the male jury, the contest was suspended. As a result of this mishap, the *Padristas* branded the *Putistas* as irresponsible and rabble-rousers, explaining that you didn't win wars with breasts.

These events deepened the gulf between the two factions, dividing once and for all families, friends, and strangers. *Padristas* and *Putistas* cut all ties, choosing to spend their time in separate places, to buy their groceries only from grocers with shared ideological views, and to make up dirty jokes about their rivals. The sisters, mothers, and grandmothers of both parties were systematically insulted and their personal hygiene habits hung out for public perusal. To better distinguish themselves, the *Padristas* began to wear red armbands, the *Putistas*, green ones. On the *Padrista* side, the padre was the natural born leader. On the *Putista* side, Madame Lola ruled the roost. While he granted indulgences, she handed out condoms.

With hatred and intolerance intensifying with each day, a sensible soul proposed a fight between the two leaders. 'I accept,' they both exclaimed, relieved that nobody had thought about organising a political debate. Specialists appointed by both parties met in secret to define the conditions and rules of the fight. Following several hours of heated discussion, threats of violence, and offers of bribery, the experts, quite sozzled and in the company of girls of dubious reputation, jointly drew up the following document:

> *To find a peaceful solution to the terrible division corrupting our society, Padristas and Putistas agree to a fight between their respective leaders. The fight will be held tomorrow at 5:00 p.m. under the following conditions:*
> *1. The venue chosen is the central square.*
> *2. To make a real show of it, the ground in the square will be watered until puddles of mud form.*
> *3. The opponents should show up unarmed and in sporting attire.*

4. There will be no referee.

5. The first to knock out his or her opponent will be declared the winner.

6. All manner of blows are admissible.

7. Ear biting will result in disqualification.

Entry is free.

On the following day, hours before the fight, the square was already packed with supporters for each fighter. The climate of expectation and uncertainty as to the outcome of the fight had brought out mankind's natural compulsion for gambling and easy profit. Illegal betting was rife: 'Five chickens on the padre to win.' 'Two cows on Lola to win.'

The first fighter to arrive was Madame Lola, accompanied by her entourage, which included her trainer, her masseur, and her shrink. Lola, dressed in a leopard-skin bikini and high-heeled boots, triumphantly entered the square, arms in the air. She was received by her fans with a huge round of applause and heckles of encouragement. 'Kill him!' they shouted. 'Skin him alive!'

Minutes later the padre arrived, joined only by his trainer (the sexton) and two masseurs (the catechists). The padre, sporting a yellow thong, football boots, and an inexplicable nose ring, warmed up by throwing punches in an attempt to intimidate his opponent, while loud applause and cries of encouragement rang around the square. 'Kill her!' 'Skin her alive!'

With the two contestants in place, the master of ceremonies grabbed his microphone. 'Ladies and gentlemen, to my right, the whorehouse whirlwind, five feet seven inches, one hundred and ninety-eight pounds, Madaaaaaame Lolaaaa. To my left, the terror of the confessional, five feet three inches, one hundred and seventy-six pounds, theeeeee padreeee.'

The first moments of the fight were spent in close and very careful mutual inspection, doing a few turns of the arena until they were giddy. The crowd was growing restless and about to let out a few jeers when the brawl began. Out of the blue, the padre took the initiative, grabbing Lola by the hair and lifting her onto his back before violently throwing her down onto the ground, letting out a roar of biblical proportions. The *Padristas* whooped and leaped with joy. The *Putistas* let out a collective 'Ooh.' Stunned, Lola got to her feet with difficulty, like a pachyderm far into its siesta being forced to stand, shooting sparks of hatred at the padre with her eyes.

The long-awaited psychological game began. Pundits believed the padre to have an advantage over Madame Lola, thanks to his experience with tortured souls, which they felt trumped the griping heard by the harlot in brothel beds.

'Did you like that? You'd best throw in the towel while you still can,' the padre called across the ring. But no sooner had he proffered these words of derision than Lola kicked him in the testicles, causing him to crumple to his knees. The fighter made the most of her opponent's faint-like state, grabbing him by the scruff of the neck and forcing his face into a filthy puddle for seconds.

'And now? Not smiling now, are you?' They were now level pegging, both in terms of blows given and suffered, and dirt inflicted.

The fight then paused for a commercial break. Young girls paraded around, holding posters advertising alcoholic drinks. Purists of the sport complained that this was absurd. Male members of the audience complained for other reasons: 'Couldn't they have gotten better chicks?'

The fight began at exactly the same point where it had been interrupted, with the priest in a muddy puddle, which seemed to confirm the Marxist theory of history repeating itself in the form of farce. With the fighter voluntarily immersed on the ground, as if 'turning the other cheek,' a little sportsmanship was expected of Lola. But, proving that in today's world there's no place for altruism and that jungle law prevails, the fighter grabbed the moment to force her booted foot down on his head and screamed victory with clenched fists in the air. The crowd froze: the *Padristas* mortified by the imminent defeat of their leader, the *Putistas* devastated that the fight could end so quickly. But then, with winning bets already being paid, the clergyman pulled himself free of Lola's heavy boot, swung around, and leapt from the ground in an acrobatic somersault.

While Lola disconcertedly scratched her chin, trying to figure out what she'd done wrong, the padre, still leaping about, caught her in the eye with a glob of well-aimed spit. The stunned organisers looked at each other in shock, ashamed they hadn't banned the slinging of bodily fluids. 'This isn't a porno movie,' they retorted. The crowd was divided on the matter. 'It even had blood in it,' said an outraged *Putista*. 'She should be used to such things,' a *Padrista* scathingly replied.

With little or no ethical or hygienic considerations, the padre dove under Lola's legs, causing her to tumble like a felled tree.

The fight was even once again.

It was then that Fidel Castro's army began its aerial invasion.

The first paratrooper to reach the ground was the only soldier to be injured. Having fallen onto the padre and Lola, they both attacked him. But then the remaining soldiers pointed their guns and forced the rest of the population to lie down on the ground. With the town taken, the first thing Commandant Marcos did was throw the padre and Lola in jail. They were clearly out of their minds *and* symbols of bourgeois domination and depravity. Both were stunned when they saw their former supporters – repentant *Padristas* and *Putistas* – insult and pelt them with rotten fruit.

The following day, Castro's soldiers knocked on every door in the town, ordering the townsfolk to attend a debriefing session at which the reasons for the invasion would be given. Once again everyone made their way to the square, this time wearing their Sunday best and the brooding air of someone who doesn't have a clue what is going to happen to him.

'Comrades, the capitalist oppression is over,' the

commandant began, holding up a finger in warning before an audience that was desperately trying to find meaning in his words. 'Starting today, the people are in charge. There will be no more landowners to exploit you, no financial speculators. All businesses will be nationalised and tax havens closed down.'

As the speech went on, the crowd grew more and more confused. 'Maybe it's not us he's talking to,' they muttered. 'This reminds me of one of the padre's sermons.' 'It would've been better if the Chinese had invaded us.'

However, all their doubts evaporated when the speaker moved on to more concrete subjects, things of common interest and general understanding. 'The land belongs to all of us now.'

This unexpected declaration struck the ears of all those present and was followed by a collective murmur that gradually overwhelmed the voice of the commandant, forcing him to speak louder to make himself heard. As the wall of whispers increased in intensity, isolating the orator's words, he found his vocal cords wavering, until eventually, like a flame in a bell jar, his voice was extinguished into silence. A few moments of great confusion followed, a tumult soldiers were unable to control with their pushing and threatening. The people then began to put the revolutionary theories into practice by issuing orders. 'No one touches my pig!' shouted one irate farmer, brandishing an imaginary hoe. This ignited the others, who protested heatedly against the proposal for agrarian reform and Castro-inspired collectivisation.

Surprised at the fanatical response from the people, who were proving more reactionary and bourgeois than welcoming, as the oppressed are supposed to be with their liberators, the commandant was experiencing the first signs of a tremendous headache. He took a deep breath and replied as sweetly and gently as he could: 'The pig belongs to the people, comrade.' (He said this while imagining himself savouring slices of cured ham.) But as he was getting ready to explain the benefits of abolishing private property and dividing up personal wealth and capital equipment, another man called out rudely, 'What about the women? Do they belong to the people too?' This raised a roar of coarse laughter. Having definitively lost their fear of intervening, the masses erupted in a chorus of spoken thoughts, revealing their innermost feelings. 'You can have my wife any time!' 'Let's get down to it then. Drop your drawers, Maria!' 'Oh, my poor daughters!'

Worn out and bad tempered, given the failure of the debriefing session, the commandant felt like ordering half a dozen men to be shot to set an example. He tried to restore order by saying the first thing that came to mind: 'From now on, pornography is banned.' This got him embroiled in an argument with the protesters, who were getting noisier by the minute.

'But we haven't got that here yet.'

'An ounce of prevention is better than a pound of cure.'

'Sorry, I'm not sure about something.'

'What is it?'

'Does a romp in the hay with the neighbour's wife count as pornography?'

'Well… not if she's a comrade. But if she's a capitalist, then yes, obviously it does.'

'And if she's neither?'

'That's impossible. Anyone who is not with us is against us.'

'That's very complicated.'

'And what about doing the five-knuckle shuffle?'

'Enough!' shouted the commandant, furious at the people's lack of discipline. 'This rabble is completely ungovernable,' he ruminated. He was at a loss as to how to deal with the chaos he had created.

In the meantime, some of the people had begun to insult each other, reviving old feuds, scoffing, and generally threatening to transform the debriefing session into a pitched battle. The soldiers, unused to such attitudes, suspected that these must be very strange and complex people, maybe even a little crazy. They hesitated about what to do. Once more, the commandant proved he could deal with the most sensitive situations with enviable *sangfroid*: two shots into the air were enough to calm people down and reduce the clamour to a deathly silence.

The square now looked as if it were filled with stiff statues modelled by an unimaginative sculptor. Dazzled by his own magic, the commandant savoured the moment, more convinced than ever that one shot was worth a thousand words.

With arms outstretched as if to embrace the crowd, he addressed the protesters again, this time with more confidence. 'I can see that I didn't make myself clear, comrades. This can all be summed up as a process of dialectic, whereby the opposition of contrary concepts gives rise to the perfect synthesis. That is to say, what used to be mine and yours is no longer mine or yours; it's now ours. Do we understand each other?'

The pig owner, who greatly appreciated sausages and brined meat, was visibly distressed and muttered: 'He won't eat pig feed.' But all others remained silent. This subtle example of popular wisdom, where silence can mean anything at all, from a given thing to its exact opposite, left the commandant wary. He then realised that facing a silent crowd could be a much more difficult undertaking than confronting a noisy mob.

Meanwhile, accustomed to simple yet incontestable language, the people were waiting to be given clear orders and specific instructions. For the selfsame reason, they became more rowdy when the commandant urged them to speak up, in what he called a session of criticism and self-criticism. 'Comrades, to perfect our new classless society, each of us will say what he or she thinks about himself or herself and about others.' This unexpected invitation was received with astonishment by those present, now entirely convinced that some sort of plot was being hatched against them.

'I told you he was a padre in disguise.'

'He just wants to know where we keep our money.'

'Anyone who speaks will be hanged.'

With the sentiment of the people explained, verbalised in collective fears, no one dared to open their mouth.

Helplessly watching as his strategy crumbled around him, the commandant controlled a new urge to draw his gun, recalling the old psychological manipulation techniques he had learned at elementary school. 'Anyone who finds his tongue gets some chocolate,' he cried, his face trapped in a satanic angelic smirk. 'Some chocolate?' the people called out, unable to contain the saliva pouring from their lips.

'Yes, some chocolate.'

'The good stuff?'

'The best money can buy.'

A huge tumult broke loose once again in the throng, with everyone jostling for position, leaping in the air and trampling on each other's feet as they struggled to be granted the right to speak. This time the soldiers, themselves deprived of the pleasure of the capitalist invention known as chocolate, had no qualms about unleashing their rifle butts on the crowds. What was the point of eating delicacies once your teeth have been bashed out? Finally, when everyone had settled down, the commandant ordered that everyone sign up to talk. To his surprise, the process was all very civil, without any insults or blows. The only break in the proceedings came with some angry voices proclaiming, 'Exploiters and the exploited will only cease to exist on the day everyone eats chocolate mousse!' 'Pastry chefs of the world unite!'

As first on the list, Jack the tanner had the honour of opening the problematic session of criticism and self-criticism. Clutching his bar of chocolate and with all eyes on him, Jack suddenly felt embarrassed and ashamed. His hands behind his back, eyes cast to the ground, like a seminarian caught masturbating, he walked in fear toward the commandant. 'Commandant, tell me what I should do.'

'Comrade Jack, say everything you think about yourself and about your comrades.'

'Everything?'

'Everything!'

'Right, well... I'm a good and honest man. As for the others, I have this to say: Manuel the grocer steals from his customers. Peter's wife cheats on him in his own home. Alfred borrows money and never pays you back. The Smith family—'

Before he could manage to complete his accusation, he was struck firmly on the head by a stone missile. A storm of pebbles then rained down, eventually hitting the commandant. Swift to reply, the soldiers unleashed a volley of shots into the air, lashing their rifle butts into the crowd once again.

Half an hour later, everyone returned to their homes, Jack and another twenty on stretchers, the commandant supported by two soldiers. The words 'criticism' and 'self-criticism' were never spoken again.

A week after these events, Fidel received the following letter from the commandant.

Comrade Fidel

In spite of our efforts to liberate this people of the capitalist oppression, our mission isn't all that easy. The problems are more complex than we had predicted. The military conquest was certainly a success, but conquering minds has proven an inglorious task. These folks are a strange bunch. They completely lack discipline, and it seems the only thing that interests them is to denigrate other people.

That said, I therefore fear that they do not fit into the traditional class-struggle scenario, and that we will have to undertake extensive research into the natives to understand and classify them.

I therefore request (although I feel this to be a lost cause) the urgent expedition of experts in exotic species and Marxism, to see if we can manage to indoctrinate this strange people.

However, to use one of their own sayings, I have the feeling that only the bristle of bayonets will work here.

Long live the revolution,
Comandante Marcos.

Sitting on a blue velvet sofa in one of his clandestine residences, dressed in little more than a pair of white shorts, Fidel Castro held the letter from Marcos in one hand, studying it, supporting his forehead with the other. Stripped of attire because of the tropical heat, he looked more like a retired athlete. The signs of exceptional physical prowess could still be deciphered to those predisposed to this archaeological task, finding in these ruins the remains of former grandeur. Thus, like a majestic temple that once held gods and astounded mortals but now only boasted a few columns, Fidel presented the attributes of every great monument: he had inspired countless books, documentaries, and films. The masses knew him, and his place was guaranteed in history.

The news that the arrival of the revolution threatened to trigger a conflict between the populations instead of causing the people to acclaim Fidel as their liberator provoked neither distress nor rage. He now knew the last battle of his life was waiting for him. Fidel became possessed by the survival instinct of a wounded, wild animal, aware of its own impending death, that attacks the first thing crossing its path. He couldn't wait for the days to come to an end, powerlessly watching as his body and mind deteriorated. As in the beginning, so in the end, he had to take the initiative.

It was around this time that Fidel got into the habit of writing down notes, his reflections, and scattered thoughts. Years later, some historians would consider them a kind of political testament, while others deemed them to be of little value, arguing that they were texts written when he was already not in full possession of his faculties.

On this particular day he wrote the following:

I admit that I have failed, as I have been unable to free the people from the animal condition to which capitalism has reduced them, breaking their will and exploiting them. When it comes down to it, a flicker of stupidity and evil will always remain in the spirit of the masses, independent of what they are taught. I put an end to illiteracy, I trained the finest technicians and specialists, I guaranteed a worthy profession to every citizen. In short, I freed them from ignorance. But to what end? So that they could revolt against me?

If I could do it all again, I would have so much to set straight!

Capitalists are more aware than anyone of human nature, of its penchant for violence, its selfishness, and its ingratitude. These bestial instincts have been instigated against the revolution for years. Thus, I've had no choice but to take radical measures from the outset. Could it be any other way? With such powerful forces against us? However, my enemies have ended up handing me the legitimate right to defend myself, resorting to methods similar to those of the former regime. How stupid they are. How shortsighted they are. Thanks to their help, I have become a type of martyr for whom everything is permitted, for whom all excesses are forgivable. When it comes down to it, all great men need great enemies. So, every time they attempted a new coup against the revolution or assassination attempt on my person, I was given the incontestable right to fight back with an iron fist against my home enemies. Do those cowards waiting in the comfort of their homes, protected in the arms of their wives while I face death, really think they can seize the power to rule the revolution? Through my example of daring and courage, for the secure leadership shown, for the altruism on behalf of millions of human beings, I am the only one who deserves the title of 'El Comandante.'

I admit some convictions have left me in doubt as to the defendant's guilt. Some innocents may have been caught in the protective web of the revolution without right to defence. However, worst of all, what hurts me the most is having been forced to make drastic decisions against former comrades-in-arms turned crazy. But what else could I do? Waver? Reveal the weakness of decision? Encourage further subversion through forgiveness? Never! The revolution is a violent and troubled process, full of mistakes and errors, permanently being fine-tuned, and thus devouring any and every threat it is faced with, its eyes shut tight, fists clenched. What do a few individuals matter when the common good is at stake? Religion, this doctrinal weapon against the revolution, which our enemies have never given up, provides the example of the need to sacrifice the Son of God for mankind in order to achieve redemption.

Then, and don't forget it, it's vital to remind the people about the severe punishment that awaits them if they dare join their enemies' games. Is there any language they understand better? A government replacing the heavy hand of scientific socialism with the dialogue of bourgeois democracy invites the executioner to his own beheading, placing the axe in his hand. If we hadn't controlled the media, an endless source for revolution propaganda and for attacking capitalism, or created police surveillance, involving citizens themselves, instructed to rat out any conspirators in their neighbourhoods or in their families, how could we have survived systematic attacks from such perfidious enemies for so many years? To crush the counter-revolution, branched out into separate factions but all conspiring to the same goal, the population had to be prepared for its self-defence. This doesn't mean half of the citizens keeping an eye on the other half, as some agitators would have it. What it means is the overwhelming majority of the people joining forces against the threat of a dangerous minority. The effectiveness of these Revolution Defence Committees, used later to carry out the noble tasks of eradicating disease, providing safety in the workplace, and reconstructing property, is undeniable proof of the support and loyalty of the citizens.

Only in a utopian society, where there is no evil or greed, could you go without the instruments of dissuasion used to assure collective happiness. This is the route we are taking and, if the journey's end is impossible to reach, we have come so much closer to this goal than the illusory societies of capitalist democracy, fraught with inequalities and injustices. Our revolutionary conquests have amazed humanity, in particular our critics, and have become a beacon of hope for the downtrodden and oppressed around the world. We are the living example of how people can free themselves from the shackles of bondage and become the masters of their own destinies. We have exposed the fraud of capitalism, outdoing its scientists and its athletes. We have ridiculed the stinginess of bourgeois charity, contrasting it with the dignity of socialist solidarity. For this reason, and this reason only, they hate us so much. We are their worst nightmare, the incarnation of everything they fear: distribution of wealth and equality among men.

If false communists shamelessly sell themselves, trying to include us in their batch of goods, betraying their people and their history, we will resist, not proudly on our own, but with the solidarity of every worker on the planet. I have discovered that in moments of greatest tension, when one is forced to keep the boat afloat through the violence of the tempest, that one experiences an indescribable, almost drug-like sensation of euphoria and pleasure. Living under threat is thus a pleasure I continually pursue.

I fully understand that the sacrifices demanded of my compatriots in recent times are terrible and that children suffer the most, without understanding why. I have thus avoided visiting elementary schools and kindergartens, something I once took great pleasure in doing. The truth is that I just can't face these unhappy generations, condemned to inhuman deprivations. I even fear that many of these unfortunate innocents will never achieve full physical and psychological development. Only my unshakeable faith in the future of revolution and the absolute certainty that there is no other alternative allows me to face this dramatic situation with serenity, in which my people prove they are ready for anything to defend the country.

But who are the real culprits behind this tragedy if not the capitalist forces who, when trying to destroy our economy, don't look at the means to justify the end? Who forces women and men of this country to sell their dignity to the vanguard of capitalism, the tourists? They do it to try and demoralise us and to weaken the future guardians of the revolution, demonstrating in their ignorant avarice that they are capable of heinous crimes against humanity.

But I do not forgive the deserters who flee to enemy countries, abandoning their comrades who, resist in stoic silence in this grave moment that demands unity and solidarity. It is true that with their cowardly escape they help purge society of harmful elements and that they will shortly start sending money to our banks. However, through their miserable example of selfishness they undermine the confidence of their compatriots, loyal to the revolution, causing them on occasion to be tempted to follow suit. Thus, given that a single traitor can lead dozens of citizens to perform the same perfidious deed, not to mention the international shame to which they subject our country and myself, it is imperative we use all means to hinder such awful defections. Everyone who wanted to leave had their chance when, in an unprecedented lesson for the enemy, which I still laugh about today, we loaded a ship with all the scum we found in prisons and a few madmen who were cluttering up psychiatric hospitals and dispatched them toward capitalist waters, claiming dissident amnesty. It was fun, but the games came to an end.

Thus, I have no regrets for having put to death some wretched beings who tried to flee. They got what they deserved and hopefully those who managed to escape the boat and aircraft patrols ended up as shark bait. But I do regret not having acted in the same way with all those who in one way or another have damaged the revolution, sowing the seeds of instability now flourishing.

I was probably too ambitious. I strove for the impossible when I dreamed that I would be able to take the revolution to the four corners of the world, when I should have restricted myself to perfecting it on my own doorstep. A huge effort came out of this pipedream, but with negative consequences of which were the following: in trying to assert myself as a world leader, travelling from place to place, I neglected my duties of ensuring the proper working of the revolution. I delegated responsibility to men who were not always of the greatest competence or integrity. For this reason, as I discovered the intellectual and ethical limitations of the servers of the revolution, their mistakes and their weaknesses, I was forced to chop away dead wood, removing my staff until there were none left, piling the burden of major decisions on myself. I now know that delegating responsibility led inexorably to treachery, bringing out the very worst in each man, awakening demons that would otherwise remain dormant. As such, I am entirely convinced that commanding a state should not be shared. Otherwise you risk individual differences and inevitable contradictions weakening the nation, leading it to catastrophe.

This is the drama of bourgeois democracies, in which opposition to the government stops it from implementing its program, forcing it to negotiate amendments to the laws that distort the spirit of the intended reform. I'll never tire of saying it, but the principal interests of the people and of the revolution require an absolute guardian. Without a strong leader to guide and protect them, kind to loyal citizens but ruthless with traitors, both loved and feared, the people feel lost and fall into barbarism. The masses are a violent creature demanding a short leash, as liable to give his life for his master as to shun him and devour itself.

How many times has my presence alone been enough to breathe new strength into weary farmhands, or workers worn out with effort?

How many times, in the most dramatic moments of our short history, has the firmness of my words lifted the morale of the frightened population?

How many times has the power of my gaze upon the masses deterred riots and treachery?

Where others resort to brute force, all I need is charisma. Socialism is the last stage of the progression of history, but it does not ignore examples from the past that teach us the importance of an all-powerful leader at the root of all great civilisations.

Although I have faced powerful forces endowed with armies able to destroy the world, perverse and fanatical minds focused on the destruction of my dream, the only opponent that could really tarnish my leadership and divert the love of the people is religion and its multitude of padres. I am very familiar with their power and their organisation as I myself received my education in the Church. Part of what I am today, I must confess, I owe to the Church. It has centuries of accumulated knowledge, a complex organisation, and an unrivalled ability to survive and to adapt to every historical period and regime. The Church is one of the most fascinating and accomplished of human creations, but also one of the most dangerous.

Created to free man from exploitation, the Church soon joined forces with the powerful when it understood that it couldn't defeat them, in an infamous alliance of material interests aimed at keeping the masses submissive through manipulation of their faith. Over time, it has cruelly eliminated rivals and imitators until becoming the dominant spiritual power of the West. It has thus ruled unopposed, strengthening its pact with capitalism to mutually benefit. Up until, that is, the birth of scientific socialism, the only ideology able to confront the Church and succeed, unmasking hypocrisy and showing people the true path toward liberation.

For this reason, when the Church realised that the days of its monopoly of souls were numbered, it armed itself as ingeniously as it could to annihilate scientific socialism. Since then the church has become one of our worst enemies, on a fanatical crusade, dragging millions of beings imprisoned by ignorance into a holy war against socialism. Exploiting the ghosts that torment the simpleminded souls, the fears that incite them to irrational violence and the petty selfishness of keeping hold of a wealth they have never owned, the Church fought furiously against us. I therefore couldn't tolerate it in my country, for the reasons given, but, above all, because its capacity for domination and alienation of the people would rob them of strengths that should be used in favour of the revolution.

The workers do not need God's intermediaries promising them heavenly paradise while engaged in their earthly bondage. What they do need is leaders able to galvanise them in the construction of a better world. The establishment of a new spiritual base for the masses would only be possible with the disappearance of the former.

The international capitalist press has abused me without interruption since the triumph of our struggle in infamous campaigns designed to sabotage the revolution, in which they compared me to criminals whose names are not worth repeating. They told stories about badly treated prisoners, deliberately confusing common criminals with political opponents, and about arrests due to crimes of opinion, omitting that they were insults and slander punishable by law, as if in bourgeois democracies prisons were hotels and courts were not heavy-handed.

And did they not persecute those who sympathised with our cause?

Not content, they fabricated a range of falsehoods, such as those linking me with the trafficking of drugs and organs, when drug addiction doesn't exist in my country and our patients receive the very latest in medical treatment. How easy it is to belch delusional rumours, vile lies, and absurd tales. In a world torn by misfortune and by suffering, they have chosen to flog our country. They inflate small problems common to any society, giving them the seriousness of crimes against human dignity. They silence astonishing achievements the revolution provides for citizens in the most varied of areas.

Why do they not compare our level of development with those of our neighbouring countries?

Why do they hide that our doctors treat patients for free?

And why do people come from capitalist nations to be treated in our hospitals?

To such provocations I have replied with serenity, inviting journalists from a range of countries to visit us and witness with their own eyes the advances achieved and the enthusiasm of the people in the creation of a new society. With capitalism unable to corrupt all its servants, the majority of these visitors, after having bombarded me with questions that weren't always pertinent, had no other choice but to tell the truth.

Would it have been any different if the great enemy had not refused to buy our sugarcane? If it had accepted the proposal of reinstating trade links?

How would the revolution have been then?

Now, so many years after this dramatic rupture, where one door closed for another to open up, it is useless to try and imagine a different history than the one that actually happened. Yes! Our history was thus and it could never be anything else.

The price all great men pay for rising above mediocrity is loneliness. In my case, this isn't just about being above the rest, but also about not being able to trust them, these two reasons forcing me into monastic isolation. While constantly changing homes is exhausting, I can't complain. Aside from preventing attempts on my life, which the capitalists have been prodigious but ineffective at, moving has saved me from having to suffer meticulous heads of department boring me with pointless reports. Moreover, as I advanced in years and the wear and tear of so many years of fighting began to show, I increasingly felt the need to rest during the day. This was an act I hid from my subordinates, so as not to give the impression of weakness. If they knew, or if they imagined the number of treatments to which I submit myself to remain alive, my detractors would say I was no longer in a state to govern and that my decisions were the product of a senile mind. The people, for their part, under the crossfire of rumours and official denials, would be seized with helpless panic, leading them to unpredictable behaviour, like dizzy cockroaches.

As such, the state of my health is the most important state secret, with its guardians aware of what awaits them if they dare betray my confidence. With their strange instruments and mysterious remedies, always serious as if a tragedy were imminent, they peer at my body, suck blood from me, and fill me with drugs, supposedly caring for my life day and night. They are the only ones to know what I do not, who take decisions without consulting me and give me orders. I know they hide some of the truth from me and that the piece of bad news they give hides another that is even worse, although I urge them to never evade the issue. Having conquered and humiliated the powerful of this world, one after the next, I end up lost in their hands in which I am nothing more than a plaything for them to open and close, to test its abilities and limitations.

I do not deny that I am tired, nor do I ignore that my time on this planet is running out, but my desire to serve the revolution, instead of fading away like a weak leader, remains as firm as rock. As a result I am incensed when some of our so-called allies try to convince me to change, to accept the pact with capitalism and to tolerate those who want to overthrow me, establishing a bourgeois democracy that would be the perfect antithesis of the revolution.

Do they think that at this time in my life I would deny my past and the entire reason for my fight?

Do they sincerely hope, as others haven't managed to do it, that I am the one to demolish the revolution?

And could I ever betray the people, who have always been ready for new sacrifices and pains?

How could I tell those who have entrusted their lives to me that I have sold myself to the enemy?

Never, in my entire life, have I ever felt so insulted!

Faced with all the evidence revealed by our system, its enemies proclaim the failure of socialism and the end of history, granting themselves the right to represent the voice of billions of human beings excluded from the plutocratic triumph. This isn't just shortsightedness; this is malicious intent. I am now convinced that the sinister capitalist conspiracy against the revolution has infiltrated everything and that today's friends are tomorrow's traitors. All I can do is fight, against everything and everyone.

History will absolve me!

On deck of one of the ships of the *Invincible Armada*, Fidel Castro was looking through an eyeglass at the azure swath of ocean, his gaze locked on the horizon at the moment in which his imagination provided him with a triumphal preview of the battle against JFK. Thus began, preceded by a speech lasting seven hours, the voyage of invasion.

After a lunch of swordfish steaks, Fidel made his way to the hold, where he found the prisoner Varadero. Knowing that Fidel's visit implied some sort of interrogation, Varadero, armed with his own sickle and hammer and ready to adapt them to new uses, decided to take initiative by being one to control their dialogue. 'I demand to know why I am imprisoned!' Fired with no warning, these words hit the stunned face of El Comandante, causing his teeth to jitter.

Surprised by the audacity of someone whose fate depended on him, Fidel threatened to shoot him.

Varadero then began to lose sight of his former commandant, as if Fidel were transforming from the mythical figure Varadero had always seem him as into another being, a flesh and blood person. Perplexed, Varadero was confronted with an old man in various stages of physical decline: his body stooped, his hair white, his skin dull and wrinkled, his eyes faded, and his voice faint. Completely at odds with his once vigorous self, Fidel's mental abilities were also in decline. He was easily confused, experienced memory loss, repeated ideas, and had difficulty reasoning. Sharing this small space with such an unfamiliar character, Varadero initially felt the shiver of strangeness slip down his spine like a frozen slug. Then, as he began to note fragility and insecurity, he accepted the arrival of compassion, bursting out from some protected secret place. The stranger who had inspired repulsion was now an infirm human being in need of care and attention. Varadero repressed the impulse to offer his hand to help steady Fidel's tired steps. He began to nod at everything he was told. At this moment the reasons became clear as to his arrest, the undertaking that had brought it about, and the announced invasion. Without answering the spy's question, Fidel revealed in great detail the reasons for the strange succession of events in which he was entangled.

Because the discovery of the underlying causes of something worrying always brings serenity, even when the problem persists, as if the pain were one of the faces of ignorance and knowledge one of the faces of pleasure,

Varadero allowed himself then also to slip into the realms of fantasy, where he devised another dialogue with Fidel Castro. A rational conversation between two enlightened men, ready to collaborate with each other to fully clarify any doubts.

'Tell me why I am imprisoned!'

'You are under arrest because I need to take every measure necessary to stop from being overthrown.'

'It means nothing to you to ruin the life of innocent people, as this makes you feel less insecure?'

'Alas, I have no other alternative. The revolution must always come first.'

'The revolution or you?'

'My person is inseparable from the revolution. One cannot exist without the other.'

'Do you believe yourself unique and irreplaceable then?'

'That's common knowledge, especially among my enemies.'

'How can you be sure that the revolution could not head in another, perhaps better direction?'

'It could, in a perfect world that will never exist. When I am dead the country will be reconquered by my enemies and by drug traffickers.'

'Do you have no faith in the ability of the people to decide their fate? Have you actually no faith in the exceptional education you have given them?'

'It'll do them little good without a leader able to guide them.'

'And what good is a leader who denies them freedom?'

'Absolute freedom can't be found anywhere. Every regime imposes the necessary restrictions for the good of the community. None of them welcomes snakes that could destroy it.'

'I'll ask you again: destroy you or the revolution?'

'Once again I reply: we are inseparable.'

'Do you see yourself as an essential dictator then?'

'I am forced to be a dictator to stop them from destroying my work.'

'How far are you willing to sacrifice citizens in favour of this work?'

'What is happening is an absolute disgrace. I am well aware of it, and I even wonder at the lack of protests. But it's too late to turn back now. As long as I am alive all necessary measures will be taken.'

'Are you aware that it is you who will destroy your work? That you'll end up resembling those that you overthrew?'

'This is the price I have to pay. My tragedy.'

Hoping to obtain information that would ensure the disloyalty of the spy, Fidel came out of the improvised cell more confused and insecure than when he entered, finding it hard to remember what had happened in the meantime.

For his part, Varadero found an inner peace only comparable to that felt in his youth when he swore to himself to serve the revolution with all his might. During this period, which now seemed like a memory taken from a film or a book, when he believed he was holding part of the lever that was moving the world, he had felt he had strength enough to break a mountain rock if Fidel has ordered it. Now, after the slow decomposition of his convictions, this vigour returned to him once again, and he was now able to break El Comandante. Indeed, he had pierced him without much effort and returned in amazement before the mountain that he had once venerated. For this reason he called another Fidel to discuss forbidden subjects tangled in his throat, the questions he always wanted to ask and the answers he always feared hearing. This imaginary Fidel seemed entirely true to him, while he considered the other real Fidel false without a doubt.

When Fidel's ships dropped anchor and he disembarked, Commandant Marcos tried his best to put on a smile worthy of an Etruscan painting to hide the fact that all was not going to plan.

The damp wind didn't help to warm up the reception either, which ended up nothing more than a reciprocal salute and the utterance of the meagre words, 'Welcome, Commandant' and, 'Good work, comrade.' Their serious faces distorted the meaning of their words. The invitation was more objective and practical: 'I will take you to your rooms in the conquered town, and then I will show you how the population sees our revolution.' A military cortege was formed, which crawled with difficulty to the almost-socialist town.

The population watched the parade of the illustrious liberator or invader – depending on the origin of the propaganda – with a curiosity similar to that inspired by accidents and disasters, unsure whether to cheer or to throw stones. El Comandante also looked at the indecisive people with great curiosity, certain of the importance of first impressions on the human mind. He thus maintained the bellicose posture that a life of fighting had drawn on his face. He raised his head like a Roman emperor parading among the barbarians, so that no doubt as to his superiority appeared in their minds. Still, he pondered the idea that no victory can be obtained through armed force alone, and that it is necessary to offer something to defeated people, to integrate them into the winning civilisation, to make them join in the successes of the revolution.

But did the natives themselves want a revolution? The possibility that they did not tormented Fidel. As Commandant Marcos had suggested in his letter, perhaps only force would work. He thus prepared himself to face an unusual situation.

Once again he saw himself forced to turn to Varadero, the man who knew the most about this country. He thus ordered Varadero to be transferred from a cell next to that of the padre and Lola, still imprisoned as a revolutionary precaution, to the building closest to his house. Once done, Varadero was brought before El Comandante, shaved and in pressed clothes, smiling and confident, arousing in him the same sensation of discomfort suffered during the interrogation on the boat trip. Feeling as if he had recovered from what he believed to be a passing indisposition, an ordinary sickness, Fidel fell into a relapse from which he could find no antidote. For his part, Varadero felt powerful, definitively free from the condition of prisoner. He was now the bearer of a formidable influence over the fragile man in front of him.

In these circumstances of inequality, such counterparts could only have an unusual conversation, incomprehensible to anyone who had not seen the radical change underway in Varadero's mind in relation to Fidel Castro.

El Comandante's request to the spy, 'Tell me about these people you know so much about, your opinion is important,' was understood as something like 'Tell me what I should do, I feel lost.' In this logical sequence, as paradoxical as this statement may sound, Varadero replied, 'If you were king, I would tell you that your reign has come to an end and that you have no successor that the nobles and the people will accept. You are somewhere between the figure of a president, a military chief, and the guardian of a collective dream. So I say to you that your time has ended and with it the altruistic character that you tried in vain to represent. Whatever the case, all that remains of your kingdom is the rubble of the architecture of a new society, a grim devastation of an ideal brought about by your own hand, a crime for which you are the main culprit. As such, the last chance you have left to reduce the misery is to abdicate from the throne and prepare to transition rule of the country to another regime.'

This judgment struck Fidel. He felt crucified on the cross of the sentences Varadero had condemned him to, each word a pointed nail. Then, aware that El Comandante was unable to reply, Varadero continued, ready to make him swallow vinegar from the sponge before sticking the spear into his heart.

'And, what better proof of your revolution's decline could there be than this suicidal war into which you throw yourself, indifferent to the resulting consequences? Let us imagine that you achieve a resounding victory in a matter of weeks. Then what? How will you persuade the losers, when you only manage to control winners through force? Your real goal is to channel the anger that rages in our country against a foreign enemy, thus deflecting the attention of the citizens from the miserable lives to which you have condemned them and, in the event you do manage to win, offering them victory as a substitute for lost dignity. Defeat is also of use. I suspect, if you don't win, you are preparing to die in battle, thus becoming a martyr of noble for all posterity. In conclusion, you have no qualms in sacrificing human lives solely to satisfy a boundless ambition, or, put in another way, the great madness that controls you.'

Fidel went outside in an agitated state, dismissing the guards who wanted to accompany him with a brusque movement. With quick steps he followed the first path he came to and quickly left the town, as if banished. His throbbing head commanded the rhythm of his legs, adding strength to his tired muscles, as if all that was left for him to do was flee. Under the intense fire of Varadero's accusation, Fidel's kinetic energy seemed endless, allowing him to advance effortlessly through the barrier of weeds he knocked down. Powerless to silence the discordant voice ringing inside him, he lost control of his movements, erupting over the creations of nature with a fury of which he would be incapable of setting against JFK. As he passed, flocks of birds fled in fear, stripping the trees of their coats of feathers. While the sky mended skin torn by the beaks of the panic-stricken birds, other beasts swiftly slunk off into impenetrable hideaways.

Without firing a single shot, Fidel conquered the natural kingdom. A trail of flattened vegetation and crushed insects, snails, and worms were the marks left by the coarse feet of Varadero trampling on his conscience. But, while the spy moved forwards and backwards, upwards and downwards, zigzagging in an endless repetition of movements, El Comandante moved in a straight line, sleepwalking further and further into unknown territory.

Fidel's enraged wanderings would have taken him on successive laps of the globe if he hadn't been brought to a halt by a stone that fate had placed in his path. The collision resulted in a fall to the ground, his head hitting a tree trunk. There was resistance to the invader after all, discreet yet effective. With mineral patience, a submerged rock had appeared over millions of years from the depths of the earth, breaking through the crust with its extremity to trip up Fidel Castro.

Lying face down on the ground, El Comandante found himself unable to get up. His body was suddenly exhausted, his mind devoid of any emotion. He could neither move nor think. Then, in the silent language with which corpses call to worms, Fidel called upon all creeping beings to come out of their burrows to explore the flavours of his rotten flesh. The ants were quicker than the other insects, manoeuvring thousands of workers in preparation for a lavish banquet. But this didn't bother the beetles, who foraged alone for food hidden in his hair. Famished birds, more prudent than insects when assessing the weakness of their victims, circled high above before launching themselves toward his dull, glassy eyes. The feast was about to begin when Fidel, convulsing as if he had been given an electric shock, brushed them off with his hands, sending some flying and crushing others. The defensive movement also fended off the aerial threat. Almost revived, Fidel slowly dragged himself away from the ants and beetles, pushing his body forward with his knees, raking the soil with his fingertips.

As he was moving, he came across a flower in the grass. The contrast with the green mass attracted him like a bee looking for pollen, changing his creeping flight towards the stalk with red petals. At first he studied it, his eye resting on the numerous details of its delicate beauty. Then he breathed in its heady perfume, allowing himself to become intoxicated with its aroma. Finally he ripped it off with his teeth and chewed on it slowly, delighting in its forbidden flavours. Inside the mouth of El Comandante, grazing every taste bud on his tongue, caressing the roof of his mouth, were the acidic leaves of an exuberant nettle bush.

Then he fell asleep.

When he awoke he couldn't remember a thing. He knew his name was Fidel but he hadn't a clue beyond that. Where was he from? Who was he? What was he doing there? The vague idea of a mission tried to form but it soon fizzled out, brushed away by the desert storms invading his mind. Small dots of light lit fleetingly in the darkness in which he was trapped, only to be extinguished. Then a viscous mass of silence spread throughout him, coating the sound of memory. His mind a stage under the yoke of a thousand brooms, he felt at peace.

He stood up and began to walk towards the sun. The glowing light stretched the shadows. Fidel inhaled the fragrances of leaves and flowers, fascinated by the variety of aromas he didn't recognise, and tuned his ears to the discovery of animals, allowing his nose and ears the task of discovering this exotic world, his eyes guiding him in crossing the light.

When he entered a wood, a distant memory of a time when he lived hidden in the mountains resurfaced in the form of a dreamlike image in which he could see himself with other men. The image was crystal clear. He could hear his own voice and those of the others. He could even understand that he enjoyed an important status, but the meaning of this memory eluded him, as if it were from another life. This didn't affect him. Nothing could disturb him. His peace of mind seemed to find the perfect environment to develop in the mists of oblivion. Then, naturally, he gave up trying to grab the tail of the information snaking through his head, the effort of finding out his identity fading into the intense pleasure of being unfamiliar with himself.

It was in this state of absolute tranquillity, verging on enchantment, almost levitating, that the monks found him, as they were picking some wild berries and mushrooms. Fidel made his way towards them with no notion of fear or danger. The figure of a tall, bearded man in the wood frightened the monks, who held staffs in their hands, preparing to confront the potential criminal. Living in isolation, far from civilisation, the monks had been forced to learn the art of defence, mastering like few others the fearsome martial art of stick fighting; thieves and wolves had learned the imprudence of attacking them at the expense of broken bones and cracked heads. A new assailant was about to be given the same lesson. In fact, while the abbot recommended that they only use their sticks to defend themselves and that they shouldn't be excessive with force, some monks never missed the chance to venture out into the woods in search of confusion and ruckus to combat their boredom.

Local gossip, prodigious in rudeness, insinuated that this was the sublimation of bestial instincts, because if women were allowed to enter the monastery their sticks would be used for other purposes.

Luckily for Fidel, these particular monks were relatively peaceful and only unleashed a thwack when all reasonable means of civilised understanding had run out: for example, when someone disobeyed their orders. So, while they tried to encircle him, eyeing him up and down, they could see that he was unarmed. They kept their sticks poised, however, ready to react. He turned out to be nothing more than a terrible-looking tramp they had never seen before.

With his memory wiped, Fidel had to rely on his intuition to warn him that he shouldn't go any further, and he came to a halt a short distance from the monks. His serene expression and innocent posture almost disarmed them. The man before them not only showed no animosity, but had also exposed himself to a shower of blows seemingly without any knowledge of the risk. They suspected he was a madman, just like so many others staying at the monastery. Some were abandoned in the wood and others were entrusted to them by their families.

They considered the madmen pure souls, beings God had freed from sin who were worthy of compassion. As such, they charitably incorporated them into their religious community, making them take part in prayers and religious services, while also charging them with the hardest farmwork and most difficult tasks. The madmen took their meals alone in a cenacle at the rear of monastery, guarded by armed monks, who locked them in their cells after dinner until the following dawn.

Seemingly contradicting the order's philosophy, these measures were justified as essential to ensure that the monks could rest and to guarantee the safety of the insane, as some of them were given to outbursts of indiscriminate fury. The most reliable therapy for serious cases involved hot baths, straightjackets, a few days in solitary confinement and, of course, plenty of blows with a stick. Following their treatment, the patients became docile and silent, as if a shell had closed around them, until the day on which they recklessly reoffended, at which point they were given the same treatment in an endless cycle of insanity and beating.

'Who are you?'

'I don't know.'

'What are you doing here?'

'I don't know.'

This short exchange was enough to prove the monks' suspicions that Fidel was another lunatic lost in the woods, a refuge all madmen sought when banished from the towns. However, had Fidel revealed his identity and his intentions – 'I'm Fidel Castro. I'm here to invade your country' – the monks' conclusion would have been no different. These men had vast experience in their field and were fed up with compulsive liars who considered themselves important historical figures, and always the same ones: Napoleon, Caesar, Fidel Castro, etc. So, given his current situation, wandering half dizzy and alone through the woods, both truth and lies became irrelevant, and the state of his mental health was decided without appeal.

Had Fidel been in his natural state and ready for some honest self-criticism, he would have been able to compare the monk's firm conviction that anyone wandering through the woods must be mad to his own firm conviction that anyone entrusted with an important mission is guilty of treachery.

Taking it as an invitation, to have some tea and blueberry pie perhaps, Fidel obeyed the order 'Come with us!' without discussion.

As Fidel passed through the door of the monastery, monks and madmen stopped what they were doing, turning their attention to the visitor. Murmurs broke their silence. The arrival of new lunatics was nothing unusual, whether under their own steam, as with this stranger, or tied to a mule, like the guest who had most recently arrived. But the bearded man who barged into the monastery's grounds on this occasion had something different about him. Given the confidence displayed, the gracefulness of his movements, and the haughtiness of his countenance, those capable of reasoning assumed him to be someone important who had fallen from grace.

His presence here clearly indicated that he was insane. But, as they scrutinised the stranger's face, they realised that they were unable to find the unmistakable traces of madness, which, without being able to define precisely, they could recognise instantly. Nobody would have dared to consider him entirely sane and responsible for his own actions, but even so, they still couldn't quite classify him as being mad. It was as if this strange man was in limbo, somewhere between reason and madness. Although vague and imprecise, like a rumour, this realisation frightened them, ill equipped as they were to deal with situations outside the careful classification of real phenomena. Fidel, as a member of an unknown species, presented unique characteristics that set him apart from humans and animals. They decided every precaution would be necessary.

Surrounded by walls, the sturdy building sparked in Fidel's mind the memory of prisons where he had exiled political opponents. Their meaning evaded him, however, and he was left at a loss as to what they had to do with him. The spark was brief, with no power to set alight the great fire. Walking across the granite-paved courtyard, he calmly received the icy glares of the monks and the restless looks of the insane, with little to differentiate him from the impassive El Comandante who inspected prisons packed with political prisoners.

As was usual, the monks took him to see the abbot for examination. The abbot ascertained how dangerous each new inmate was, and pried him for information about his possessions. Aggressive nutcases were not given farming implements. Those who could bequeath something to the monastery were given light duties. Lastly, simple idiots were given work that no one else wanted. The rules were simple and final. With a little imagination, many similar examples can be found in the Holy Scriptures.

The meeting took place in the library, where Athanasius, the abbot, was studying the David, Uriah, and Bathsheba love triangle from a new perspective. This biblical tragedy, in which a woman whose only sin was being beautiful became the victim of a divine punishment aimed at the king of the Jews, seemed to demonstrate that the God of wrath in the Old Testament was truly a cruel fellow.

What left Athanasius confused was that Uriah's loyal attitude led him to death in battle. Being the cuckold wasn't enough, he also had to die. David seemed kind when he said that Uriah could go to his wife. Or maybe he was just being cynical. He had already impregnated her, after all. But, in the end, given Uriah's refusal to leave his troops, David was unable to resist sending him to war, thus showing his Machiavellian nature. On the other hand, Uriah showed conviction in his principles, the ability for sacrifice and enormous courage from the outset, but he died as a result.

Faced with this anything but edifying scenario, without even daring to address the relentless logic of divine justice, the abbot feared that some readers would interpret what happened as proof that noble sentiments only complicate matters, sometimes fatally, while selfishness can save us from great problems, and even save our lives. After all, if Uriah had decided to desert and run into the arms of his wife, not only would he not have died, but he would also have avoided the terrible divine punishment befalling her son. To make matters worse, as if this were compensation, David ended up marrying Bathsheba, thus achieving his insidious plan. The moral of the story, the abbot thought uneasily, is that the good man who leaves his family to serve his country loses everything, while the bad man, despite being brought to justice, ends up profiting from his perfidy. This reasoning worried him. David, Uriah, Bathsheba – what a muddle they were in.

Couldn't they have solved it all differently? David could have lost his throne as punishment, Athanasius daydreamed, trying to rewrite holy history. Uriah could have been seriously wounded only to recover and return to the beautiful Bathsheba, the couple living happily ever after with their legitimate and illegitimate children, some blond, some brunette, in a show of great tolerance.

He was lost in these thoughts, retouching punishments and introducing rewards, ensuring that nobody had to die, and giving a bit more clarity to the definition of good and evil and their respective consequences, when the arrival of a new lunatic was announced, forcing him to put a halt to his cogitations. Having to interrupt his train of thought just as it was bearing flowers and forbidden fruit left him exasperated. The abbot was just preparing to unleash his wrath on the monks and the madman, when he was faced with the singular figure of Fidel Castro.

He fell silent, gulping down the words that had been forming in his mouth, his fury evaporating in an instant. Raising his hand, he silenced the monks before they could explain the presence of the man they brought before him. The abbot walked full circle around Fidel and stood right before him, as if challenging him to react in some way. Fidel, absorbed in his attempts to decipher the incomplete sketch chalked in his mind, smiled absently. For a few moments, Athanasius almost believed that he was looking at JFK's fearful enemy. The supposition, being absurd, gained in consistency and clarity as he confirmed the incredible similarities between the mad stranger and Fidel Castro. However, all that was needed was a fleeting expression from the creature, a brief spark of soul, nothing more, for his suspicion to go up in smoke. At first the proof disheartened him, like a diamond miner discovering that his sieve contains nothing but worthless stones. Then he felt irritated again, furious at having been both instigator and victim of fraud. Finally, his hands behind his back, he recovered his composure and said to the guards, 'Who is this poor devil?'

'We don't know. He doesn't either.'

'Who are you?'

'I don't know,' replied Fidel, disturbed by the inner turmoil that this question was beginning to unleash.

'Who is your family? Where do you come from?' the abbot tried again, hoping to find a loaded looney.

This question made Fidel's face muscles contract, crumpling his lips, as he was suddenly bombarded with inaccurate images of his country, detonating familiar voices and aromas. The flood of reminiscences left him restless. His mask of beatitude broke and a new face was revealed. Without either of them knowing it, El Comandante looked at Athanasius as he would have done an impertinent subaltern, forcing him to lower his head in a sign of submission. And it was thus, with eyes to the ground, that the abbot, furious at what was happening to him but powerless to avoid it, classified Fidel Castro as a dangerous, insane amnesiac, instructing the monks to never place farming implements in his hands and to watch him day and night. Listening to his diagnosis and sentence, the monks performed a ceremonial bow and grabbed Fidel by the arms. They had already opened the library door when Athanasius said, 'Wait! Leave him here!'

The madman was nonetheless an enigmatic being, a force Athanasius feared was greater than he. This left him worried. Athanasius needed to know more about this man, to look inside his soul, to discover some hidden weakness. But how should he proceed if the creature seemed to be unaware of his own identity? This required tact and consideration, notable qualities of which he believed he was well stocked.

He then had an idea. What if he questioned him about something or other? After all, it is when expressing their opinions that men expose the foundations of their mind, peeling back the paint and plaster under which can be found clues to who they really are. A vile and mean character, no matter how well disguised, can suddenly be revealed. A pure soul might emerge from a crude and repulsive figure.

To loosen the stranger's tongue he would begin by discussing a random subject and then ask him some questions. But what would he discuss? From what he had witnessed thus far he excluded one subject – football. Who could tell if, on hearing nothing more than the word 'club,' Fidel wouldn't start to rip the library's entire collection to pieces? Because of the constant ruckus between monks whenever they discussed football, he had been forced to ban supporters, scarf wearing before the games, and teddies. In his opinion, if football had existed in Roman times and there had been a tournament with teams from every conquered territory meeting in the Colosseum, East playing West, (un)friendly games against Carthage, slaves skilled in dribbling freed, referees thrown to the lions every week, incoherent debates in the senate between patricians, Apollo and Augustus represented wearing football boots, temple columns serving as goal posts, baths invaded by footballers, the empire would not have lasted half as long as it had lasted. The barbarians would have found nothing but the ruins of Rome, and the Christian religion would have been extinguished.

While studying the impenetrable face of Fidel Castro, Athanasius wondered what topics of conversation would be likely to spark curiosity in this listless mind. In any common man, with no particular interest in anything apart from women or the problematic subject of football, the chances of success were very high. In this man, without knowing the motivations guiding him, he suspected that this rule did not apply, nor any other that he could think of. With his finger trembling over the trigger, he would have to risk a shot in the dark towards a target that might exist, exposing himself to the skewed fury of a probable ricochet.

It was thus, with Fidel in his sights, that he shot the story of David, Uriah, and Bathsheba at point-blank range, without knowing how to explain the reasons behind choosing such a biblical projectile. The story was told slowly, as if to allow the full absorption of events, with lavish details about the atmosphere of the period and the physical appearance of the protagonists, with Bathsheba receiving the favours of his artful imagination. As he spoke, he could clearly see the faces of the two rivals, bearded like Fidel, the moral dilemma facing them both (he believed that David was also tormented by the decision), almost convincing himself that the blame lay entirely at Bathsheba's feet, a wicked woman unable to resist the seductive arts of the king of the Jews and the temptations of the flesh. Just think what this woman would be capable of nowadays for money and fame. She'd take part in televised talent contests, candidly reveal herself in women's magazines, maybe even write a blog. But shortly afterwards, remorseful of his shameful chauvinistic snub, he pondered how a simple plebeian, educated to submit to the stronger sex, certainly illiterate and without plumbing in her home, could dare turn her back on the most powerful man in her community.

He was right back to square one, unable to draw any conclusions. Far from discerning an objective moral meaning with a clear definition of good and evil, the story was like a painting deprived of perspective. The distant figures oversized and the close figures small, created to befuddle the onlooker, susceptible to free interpretation. Maybe the Creator, like all creators, enjoyed breaking free of stereotypes now and then, subverting the rule and breaking with tradition to produce something that only much later – and by the looks of it, a couple of millennia was not enough – would be understood. Divine and human nature was that complex.

In telling the story, Athanasius hoped to spark the mysterious man's interest. Perhaps Fidel would comment on the story and show a glimpse of his personality. After all, maybe other mental tools, even if hardly compatible with the mechanisms of concrete reality, would be needed to interpret such a painting. Didn't all scholars look a bit crazy and have long beards?

Told countless times to assemblies of children in the Jesuit college he had attended, almost always with the burden of guilt given to Bathsheba, as David was a biblical star who specialised in stone-throwing duels (and heroes were permitted certain weaknesses) the story sounded familiar to Fidel, helping him to ascend one more step up the staircase to memory and identity. Without realising it, Athanasius had revived the dying spirit of El Comandante, who, stimulated by the electric shocks of the remembered words, responded with sudden quivers in an intermittent awakening of consciousness. This internal process became visible on the exterior, revealing itself in Fidel's increasingly gloomy expression, in his deep breathing, in his fingers passing through his hairy chin.

When the abbot finished his tale, words escaped from Fidel's mouth. 'This fictitious story is a good example of the abuse of the elite on the working classes, of the use of religion to legitimise the excesses of the powerful, and of the systematic punishment of women in imperfect societies that have yet to reach the superior level of scientific socialism. David is a despotic monarch whose wealth lies in the exploitation of an oppressed people who are deprived of access to education. He resorts to the brute force of the army and to the legitimating arguments of priests so that he can remain in power. His depravation leads him to seduce a married woman of lower social standing. He then conjures up a strategy that will see him freed of her husband.

'Like all exploiters of the working classes, he is a vile and unscrupulous character.'

'Bathsheba represents the housewife looking after the household while her husband is away serving the tyrant, a domestic worker. She has spent her life scrubbing steps and washing dishes and clothes. She has never danced across the ballrooms of high society. Bathsheba is corrupted by David when he seduces her, promising her wealth. Her act of infidelity shows how capitalism perverts the people when the people do not have an ideological foundation to resist it. She is thus the main victim of this story.'

'Uriah is also a member of the people who for the same lack of indoctrination loyally serves the tyrant, convinced that their interests coincide. Thus, even if for different reasons, he is not only wronged by Bathsheba but also by David. But, unlike his wife, he resists the temptation, not of wealth but of being back with his family, revealing an integrity of character only possible in the humble. His death in combat serving the man who took his wife is an allegory of the depredation of the oppressing classes on the workers, dispossessed of their possessions, their loved ones, and their very lives. In this immoral tale we prove the bloodthirsty nature of capitalism, its dependence on the illiterate, and the need to educate the people to overthrow despots.'

Athanasius was mesmerised, stunned, and stranded. His prayers had been answered: the stranger had revealed who he was and the biblical mystery seemed to be solved. *This guy can only be Fidel Castro. I dont know how he got here, but it's him. I'm certain of it,* he reflected euphorically. *Nobody can learn of this. The best thing is to keep it secret and then I'll see what use it could hold.*

The abbot now dreamed about the lessons in leadership and strategy that Fidel could give him, so that he could later present himself as the saviour of the nation. Who knows, he could maybe even become pope. So many years looking after crazy people and not once had anyone noticed his humanist qualities. Nobody had promoted him or invited him to take

on an important ecclesiastical post. He whined that having
no sponsors was his only flaw. But now, finally, the chance to
make things right had come. Whether by divine providence or
straight out of hell, he held the skeleton key that would open
every door, and it was ready to use as per his ambitions.

That night Fidel slept in a comfortable cell, enjoying similar
amenities to those of Athanasius. It was quite different from
the damp cubicles infested with bedbugs of the insane. When
they woke him at dawn to take breakfast together with the
monks, he had no idea where he was, and he began to wonder
what he was doing there.

These thoughts led once again to the disturbing matter of
determining who he was. As he chewed, he didn't notice the
taste of the freshly baked bread, and he paid no attention to
the warm words spoken by the abbot. Instead, he rummaged
through random recollections, trying to fit them together.

In one of the jigsaw pieces, he was leading the attack on
a city, firing on a fenced-in army barracks. In another he sat
in a luxurious mansion, dining alone under the cold light
of chandeliers. In a third he was giving a speech in a large
building filled with men wearing headphones. He could
clearly distinguish each of them, restless with emotions that
ranged between fear and euphoria but unable to articulate
their feelings into a coherent whole. Could he be a fighter, a
hermit, and statesman all at the same time? And if he could
choose one of these apparent identities, which one would he
go for? The possibility of leading a military revolt, whatever
or whoever it was against, and to seize power excited him. To
be listened to by hundreds of important-looking people left
him feeling flattered. However, nothing pleased him about the
loneliness revealed in the disturbing memory in which he was
in a world apart from other humans. Yes, he did not care about
being a conqueror, about triumphing over evil enemies and
replacing them in power, just as it didn't bother him to enjoy
the privilege of spreading his word throughout humanity.
However, he would never want to be confined in voluntary

reclusion, fearful of invisible threats. But – and this doubt tore him apart – were these recollections true or just the fruit of a fertile imagination? And could he rub out all of his memories, the true and false ones, delete his past and become another person, begin with nothing, like a newborn child?

These meditations withered in him during the rest of the meal. His silence greatly frustrated the abbot, who increased his stimuli and tricks aimed at loosening Fidel Castro's tongue in vain. This happened before the incredulous eyes of the monks, who succumbed to the sin of envy and pride. To them it was incomprehensible for a lunatic, even if this one wasn't entirely mad, to sit at the table with them, the masters. So, with the fear of someone who knows he is committing an act of grave disrespect, they glared at Athanasius, spewing criticism and disapproval, demanding a soothing explanation. The abbot ignored them, with no arrogance intended, unaware of the general indignation they felt, absorbed as he was in the impossible task of re-establishing contact with the man who would change his fate. Fidel, the bone of contention, was imagining storming the monastery.

When the meal was over, he was taken by the abbot to visit the monks and lunatics while they performed their farming duties, solely as an observer and without being given any task. The night before, the monks had been given strict orders not to disturb Fidel and to allow him to go wherever he wanted, so long as he didn't escape. Proudly, Athanasius explained to him in a scholastic manner the theory behind the work therapy designed to cure the insane and hinted at the happiness, unclear to a layman in the field, they felt when working like beasts. 'The only flaw in this treatment is that it has to be given for life. Stop it for a single day, even a few hours of rest, and there are serious relapses,' he explained. Fidel then saw a group of madmen digging, and further on, another group picking fruits in the plantations, under the orders of monks who, according to the abbot, had little talent for calligraphy or for illumination, or heads for studying the very complicated holy texts.

At the expense of intense muscular effort, the men using hoes struck gashes in the ground, raising the implements above their heads as if they were preparing to strike a deathblow. The action was repeated again and again, rhythmic and synchronised, with the impact of the blows on the earth producing a telluric sound of muffled drums. Commanding the large band, using a stick as a baton, were three hardworking maestros. The potato pickers studied the ground, backs bowed, some on their knees, sticking their hands in the dark earth to uproot the tubers. As if trampled by horses, the ground was churned and rutted as they passed, as it would remain until the next planting. Without going over the top, the monks accompanying them also harvested a few potatoes to escape the tedium of a day's work measured by the apparent movement of the sun.

The incident that would change the history of the monastery forever then took place. It was midday and the sun beat down mercilessly on the backs and shaved heads of the mad workers and their supervisors. Sweat flowed, and resistance was diluted. The monks' brains cooked while the brains of the lunatics, being cooked already, roasted. A chorus of groans and complaints were joined by percussive thuds on the earth, combining to produce a kind of slave-like march. Suddenly, an old madman raised his tool, held it there for a fleeting instant, and then dropped to the floor. The two nearest monks wasted little effort in trying to revive him, opting as they did for a good old thwack on the back.

Before the other monks could arrive on the scene and add their own first aid skills, Fidel had already disarmed one of the clubmen, tearing his stick from his hands before whirling around and hitting the other's arm, forcing him to drop his staff. The treacherous intrusion of the mysterious stranger left everyone stunned. He had, in a trice, rushed to the scene of the aggression, robbed the weapon from the hands of an expert, and put another out of combat without suffering a scratch.

One monk was left standing, petrified but intact. Another was on the ground, kneeling with a broken wrist. With the staff held in his hands, Fidel impassively looked around him, like a samurai, ready to face any attack.

None of the clerics dared to disobey when he summoned them to take the dying madman to the infirmary.

Then, once again, an unexpected torrent of words erupted from Fidel's mouth, but this time he felt the intense flavour of each sentence spoken, the powerful aroma of its content. 'Comrades, resist the oppression and raise arms to overthrow the tyranny. From today the time of exploitation and maltreatment, as demonstrated by this brutal aggression against your comrade-in-arms, is over. You are the productive force that is feeding society, and those who shackle you rely on your will. Change is in your hands. Remove the leech and build a new world where the sun shines on everyone. United you will never fall!' A dove flew down and perched on his shoulder.

The monks and madmen were still digesting what had happened, divided in their opinion as to who played the hero and who was the villain, but unanimous as to the rare quality of the show and the martial arts prowess of the protagonist, when Athanasius decided to prolong the entertainment, moving the onus from surprise to scandal. Just like Fidel, he spoke without thinking, although unlike his counterpart, his intentions were clear and prepared. 'Brothers, this man is Fidel Castro in disguise. Take him at once!'

You couldn't confuse the monks more if you tried, these simpleminded souls with little backbone for philosophical bombshells and more interest in good food and wine. The abbot's statement only deepened the suspicion aroused the day before, from the fatal moment when the abbot had seated the almost-madman at his table, that their superior had also lost the plot. After all, living with such an assorted array of insane specimens, some who heard voices, others who had visions, some who thought they were figures from history sent down from heaven, and even the Creator himself, ended up contaminating the mental health of anyone. Two lunatics, both claiming to receive important messages from above, one appealing for peace, the other for war, had been part of the monastery's order in the past, but no lunatic, not even the most pious, had ever managed to be promoted to the status of monk.

So, while Athanasius screamed for his orders to be obeyed and Fidel Castro remained vigilant, they realised, comparing the expression of unhinged fury of the prelate with the deformed faces of the violent madmen nearby, that this was really, recalling a diagnosis the abbot has once made, a case of madness with no possible cure. In the midst of the fuss, Fidel lowered his staff, returned it to its owner, and retired to his room. Many pairs of eyes followed him, each indistinguishable between normalcy and madness.

That night two uprisings, both violent, took place: that of the monks against their superior and that of the madmen against the monastic yoke.

The first occurred following a general meeting of the monks, featuring heated discussion on how best to dethrone the abbot. One moderate faction (the Doves), argued for the delivery of a polite letter demanding his immediate resignation. The other, more radical (the Falcons), believed it made more sense to knock him about a bit and arrest him. The moderates won by a slender majority, with the radicals managing to introduce some changes to the initial text, which, following the said changes imposed by the falcons, read thus:

Dear Brother Superior,

It has come to our attention that recently, due no doubt to enormous earthly and heavenly responsibilities, your health has suffered greatly. Your sacrifice rivals that of the martyrs of the faith of early Christianity, but even a holy man like you needs to rest so as not to enter paradise prematurely. For this reason, concerned as we are for your well-being and for the future of our humble community, we ask you to give up the difficult burden of running the monastery, allowing this tricky task to pass into the hands of another less tired brother.

Signed: The monastic militia.

Tucked under the door to his quarters, the letter slid toward the abbot's feet where it was picked up, opened, read, ripped up, spat on, and thrown in the trash. This was the sequence of events that fate reserved for the piece of paper chosen by the rebels to overthrow their superior. If the surprise at the intrepid entry of an envelope in his room was great, the indignation after having consumed its contents was much greater. Struck by the lightning of a letter, Athanasius flashed with considerations. An attempted coup d'état within his monastery. *What has this all come to? Where will it all end? What do they actually want? To establish a revolutionary leadership? Ban habits? Admit women?*

His men had gone mad, and it was entirely Fidel Castro's fault, this compulsive revolutionary who aspired to seize his power. From the first moment Athanasius had seen him, he had understood at once that he had come in stealth, to take possession of his powers and his job. Initially this thought infuriated him, encouraging him to think up some cruel revenge, but, little by little, he was convinced that Fidel had chosen him for a significance he was unaware he possessed, and this realisation filled him with vanity. All things considered, of all the places to start a revolution, the ill-fated Fidel, upon great reflection no doubt, with maps spread out on his desk and a globe prickled with pins, had chosen his monastery. What an honour!

He didn't know whether to hug Fidel or slap him.

Now, more than ever, he had to form an alliance with Fidel Castro. Together, these two great visionaries would be unbeatable. He could already see himself sitting on the majestic papal throne, covered in brocade, issuing charters, excommunicating whomever he felt like, naming a new saint. Then, as always happens in great epics, the more intelligent of the two would see himself freed of the other.

As to the monastic ultimatum demanding his resignation, this no longer worried him, certain as he was that it was no more than a sign of youth, probably an excess of testosterone that a collective slap on the wrist would remedy without further consequences. Maybe it wasn't a bad idea to identify the gang leaders who led the sheep astray, endowing them with some kind of dementia that would explain this behaviour. Paranoid schizophrenic insubordination, for example, would justify their classification as dangerously insane. But he would have to prevent future rebellions by adopting dissuasive measures. If it didn't cost too much, he would install tapping devices in every room in the monastery and place video cameras in the corridors. If God was all-seeing and all-hearing, without ever being down here to solve the problems created by mankind, then, with all due respect, behaving like a fearless voyeur, why couldn't he do the same? Only within his own domain, of course; no peeping on girls in the shower. Wasn't it up to him to maintain order and put up with hassle?

Meanwhile, the monks were tensely waiting for the abbot to reply, heatedly discussing the measures to adopt, depending on their superior's attitude. Without realising it, Fidel's speech against them to the insane had become ingrained in their heads, inoculating the virus of sedition. However, like all converts to a new faith – religious or political – the main message, deformed by the echoes of ancient belief, came to them distorted, tailored to their fears and their ghosts.

The radicals denounced the abbot's exploitation of the monks, the privileges he had obtained, and the spiritual decadence of the monastery, concluding that only seizure of power by force would put an end to such immoderation. They defended the creation of a monk committee, elected by a show of hands, to run the monastery; a cultural revolution eradicating former practices that would extend even to the insane (not that they would stop undertaking the harder tasks) and the formation of a farming cooperative with five-year plans to increase production. Their enthusiastic speech excited half of the audience, who cried out and burst into frenzied applause, while the other half just clapped apprehensively.

The moderates repeated the complaints about being exploited and oppressed by the abbot, reproaching his lavish lifestyle and admitting that the monastery's spiritual zeal had seen better days. They concluded, however, that a peaceful transition of power, free of violence, was the only path they, as messengers of peace among men, should follow. They proposed the democratic election of a new abbot using a secret ballot; the division of duties according to each one's merit (according to this logic, the insane would continue to perform the same tasks); the opening of the monastery to the public in return for payment of an agreed-upon amount; and also the hiring out of madmen to farmers in need of cheap labour. They warned, however, of the danger of revolutionary excess, and of the need to maintain order and avoid chaos, calling for respect of tradition and of heritage. The moderates' speech provoked no excitement among the other monks but managed to arouse some loud clapping from its supporters, as well as some jeering and accusations of being counterrevolutionary.

Prudently, both Falcons and Doves saw fit not to make any allusions to ending their celibacy and similar immoralities – revolution, yes siree, all well and good, but there are limits to everything. Another taboo subject was what would happen to the abbot once removed from his post.

They were thus in the thick of colluding and conspiring when the insane rebellion broke out. One of the madmen, making the most of the guards' absence and the excitement of the revolutionary meeting, had managed to escape from his cell and had freed the other lunatics. As neither balance nor coherence is of interest to the insane, with continuously changing ideas coming thick and fast and not a sane mind to be found, no plan was agreed upon. Armed with the courage only insanity allows – that proven weapon of mass destruction – they advanced wildly along the galleries toward the monks, like circus animals chasing their tamers. Although they were now in a part of the monastery they had never been allowed to see before, they soon found their bearings, guided by the sounds of monastic conspiracy. A hush fell over the group, to better follow the path indicated by their ears. The closer they got, the more relaxed their gait became, until each step was no more than a gentle brush on the granite slabs. Without a single instruction being given, and no leader to give it, the weaker allowed the more corpulent to push past, grouping at the rear of the attacking column while the latter gathered at the front. The lunatic offensive was thus formed with just a smattering of military reasoning. Finally, they ran into the hall in which the monks were meeting.

Although it is not possible to grasp how each of the madmen interpreted Fidel Castro's subversive message, given such diverging personalities and illnesses, the call from El Comandante stirred the stagnant waters of submission, forcing them to face the turbulent waves of rebellion.

Up until then, they had accepted the established order and the roles they were given to perform. Their fits of rage against the monks were momentary impulses with no other purpose than blind aggression. Then, something had changed in their demented noggins. If the concept of oppression, intuitively unclear and abstract as it may be, had existed, then from this moment it gained momentum and form, becoming visible and palpable for every lunatic. They were the victims of the monks. However, this important step forward would have only served to increase their anger if another complementary progress, certainly never imagined by the lunatics except in their dreams, hadn't been achieved. They could free themselves from bondage.

Yes, this was the major piece of news brought to them by Fidel Castro. The good tidings of the madmen, the light in the lunacy. With this ray of hope, all they needed now was to work out how they could gain their freedom, while the monks held staffs in their hands. The answer was simple. The lunatics would join forces.

Given this complex mental process, this rare psychic metamorphosis, had not El Comandante been in the state that he was, he would have called this rebellion the emancipation of the people.

Just like in the movies, the lunatics didn't announce their arrival by knocking on the door. They kicked it down instead, throwing themselves on their class enemies. Experiencing the lunatic revolution before putting their own revolution into practice, the monks were paralysed with surprise, caught at the very moment in which they were discussing the abbot's fate, unable ever to imagine that two revolutions could happen on the same day. Silent until that point, the crazy mob screamed at the top of their voices as they attacked the petrified and speechless conspirators, kicking off the fray with a considerable advantage. As in every beating session, tradition was respected. The lightning entrance of the attackers was followed by the respective diving on the enemy, fighting and scrambling as they rolled on the floor. Punches and kicks were inflicted and received, as were some headbutts, some violent hair and beard pulling, sputum and spitting, kneeing in the testicles, flying chairs and tables. Despite half a dozen monks being put out of fighting action immediately, victims of the lawless violence of the insane, little by little the monks managed to regain ground, leaving an equal number of lunatics prostrate. Even without being armed with their fearful staffs, the monks were still thick-skinned warriors. Although it is said that an enraged madman has the strength of ten men, this isn't always true as proved to be the case with the revolutionary insane. To make matters worse, two of the lunatics, probably too stunned by Fidel's message, began to fight each other. Meanwhile, the battle raged on. A monk strangled a lunatic. Two lunatics kicked a fallen monk. Other contenders threw punches among themselves with little talent but a great deal of commitment.

The racket eventually reached Athanasius's room, waking him from a deep sleep. As often happens with someone woken against his will, the abbot was immediately plunged into a bad mood, taken with a sudden anger in need of release. Like the lunatics before him, he directed his steps toward the commotion, ready to dispatch the lesson he had prepared for the rebellious monks earlier than planned. *Imbeciles!* Not content with writing revolutionary letters, they dared to disturb his sleep. *They will all be given a thrashing,* he thought, unaware that this was already happening. (The Lord does indeed work in mysterious ways.) Dressed in robe and slippers, gritting his teeth and clenching his fists, stick in hand, he decided they must be having another argument about football. *What else could it be?*

When he opened the door, the spectacle that met him did indeed resemble a discussion about football, between the monks, with one important and astonishing difference. The lunatics were taking part too. Fed up to the back teeth with football, and wanting to take his annoyance out on someone regardless of their beliefs or mental capabilities, he let loose a thwack with his stick. The first to be hit were lunatics, but shortly thereafter he reached the monks. Stunned, they soon set arms to defend themselves against this new assailant. Out of the initial battle a new, more complex battle was formed: lunatics against monks, and sometimes lunatics in cahoots with monks against the abbot.

It was at this very moment, with revolution and mental health blurring into one, that Fidel Castro appeared. A huge muddle of people, the confused ruckus brought pleasant and painful memories to his mind: the tumult of the attacks on the former dictator's forces, people coming out onto the streets in great excitement, the revolutionary ferment; but also the demonstrations of discontent with his regime, order overturned, and the imminent overthrow. Fidel understood that he was pulling images from both his past and present.

The answer to the question of his identity was on the tip of his tongue. However, he was still unable to make the final connection, because whenever he persevered in recovering these memories, they always faded, leaving behind an empty space, with no references, in which he lost himself again.

Fidel's appearance had an impact on the fighters that no hit could ever have achieved. They were embarrassed like children discovered by their fathers committing a shameful act. The fighting stopped at once, each trying to disguise his involvement as best he could. He watched scenes unfold that would have been unthinkable seconds before or hours later. Monks held out their hands to lunatics to help them up. Lunatics ruffled monks' hair. Athanasius hid his stick behind his back. The comical reconciliation caused great mortification among the monks and in the abbot, repentant for the various acts they had committed on that terrible day. The monks were no longer sure if the abbot had lost his reason. After all, he had foreseen the event and had acted at the right moment. They were unsure of the need for a revolution with unknown consequences. In fact, both the falcons and the doves were aware of having announced their proposals for revolutionary government without great conviction. Wouldn't it make more sense to live a peaceful life than risk condemnation to hell's fires?

Athanasius knew perfectly well he had gone too far, despite being unable to deny the pleasure that punching his subordinates had given him. There had to be a better way of exercising his authority over the monks and the lunatics. And as to the hope of conquering power using Fidel Castro, this now appeared an absurd dream. Just like the monks, he would prefer the peace and quiet of the monastery to the jungle outside. As to the tamed lunatics, they seemed to have forgotten the reasons for their rage. The attack on the monks was no more than an animal impulse they had difficulty in grasping, the echo of Fidel Castro's message now faint in their minds.

And so they all returned to their quarters without daring to face Fidel, who in turn watched them without knowing whether to consider them heroes or traitors. Athanasius waited until the vanquished fighters had left before going up to Fidel. 'Let us talk, dear friend.'

Once again the two men met face-to-face in the library, not to discuss biblical enigmas, classless society, and women's emancipation, but rather so that the abbot could find the peace of mind he'd lost when Fidel entered his life. Athanasius began the conversation. 'Your time in this monastery has sown discord and given rise to that disgraceful scene, and nevertheless, you are not to blame. You did no more than awaken the consciences of the lunatics and provide the monks with the reason they needed to overthrow me. Even without knowing for sure who you are, you still have the power to subvert, against which even I proved powerless. I thought that together we could have achieved great things, but I was wrong. You have a different mission.'

Without being able to explain it, Fidel felt pleased by Athanasius's words. 'I don't understand what you are saying, nor do I understand what I am doing here, but of one thing I am certain. They will rebel once again. All men end up rebelling,' he said.

'They won't if you leave…' Athanasius replied, as if pleading.

Before leaving, Fidel went to see the lunatics, who of their own free will had returned to their cells, after having their battle wounds treated by the monks, like missionaries caring for orphans. Although both revolutions had failed, and unrestrained violence had broken out, a sense of mutual brotherhood still hung in the air, a humanitarian rapture putting their basest instincts into a stupor. Without suspecting it, and with its effects probably vanished by the following day, the rebels had achieved another revolution without the need for force, deposing their demons and their bestiality.

Fidel captured this fleeting moment, this peaceful

coexistence between men at odds with each other. He had experienced it in dreams; he had destroyed it in reality. But he could not ignore the anguish caused by the disjointed memories of protests and hostile demonstrations. He found it increasingly taxing to maintain any sense of well-being and tranquillity, driven away by incessant threats.

He ordered the guards to open the doors, and he was obeyed as if he were the only authority within the monastery. When the lunatics lined up before him with the precision of a military parade, once again he was torn between admiration for their courage to revolt and contempt for daring to dethrone the lord of the monastery. He managed to put himself in their shoes, but he felt sympathy for the abbot. He felt like saying something, some sort of praise or reprimand; he wanted to praise while reprimanding, or reprimand while praising, but once again, he felt empty and unable to speak. However, little by little, the horror of disobedience turned into a massive flow of indignation where the vague tributary of libertarian wrath was diluted.

Saving him from embarrassment, the madman who was assaulted while farming the previous day spoke up, apparently on behalf of the others. His dull and faded eyes now glowed with inner life, this illuminated psyche guiding him to Fidel as if he and the group of lunatics had accompanied him since the beginning of the revolution. 'Give us your order, Comandante!'

The phrase entered Fidel by the throat, plummeting violently into his stomach. Then it spread throughout his body, burning veins, perforating muscles, cracking bones. Depending on its route, it drew grimaces of pain or scowls of suffering until it ran into his brain and his physical torture was transformed into a buzzing in his head. Then, as if endowed with tiny hands, he patiently recovered the broken pieces, glued them together, found the cut connecting wires, and reconnected them. At last he opened the closed windows and the light entered.

Fidel was found wandering on the beach, his guards having escorted him to town, without a single question being asked, or answer given. The incident of El Comandante's disappearance was considered a state secret, and thus banned from being mentioned under penalty of treason punishable by firing squads. On this same day, fancy theories and dirty anecdotes were invented to explain the event. After a night of deep sleep, like a soul returned to a lifeless body, Fidel's identity emerged from the depths in which it had hidden and memories swept over him in a brutal avalanche of past. He felt uncomfortable and confused, as if awakening from a long hibernation. The feeling had something strange had happened pursued him for weeks.

It was dawn when Fátima was woken by the phone ringing. She growled a few unpleasant words, whacked the pillow twice, but then realised a call at this time of the day must be something really important. Maybe it was God himself. So she pushed the sheets back with a kick of her feet, dishevelled fished her dentures from the glass of water, and got up, dragging her nightdress in the race to the telephone.

'Hello.'

'Fátima, it's me, God.'

'Hallelujah.' God couldn't tell if this exclamation was to make amends for his delay or just spontaneous joy.

'My son and I were thinking about the JFK-Castro war and we came to the following conclusion. Despite promising each other that we wouldn't meddle where we weren't asked to, although the risk of failure could mean the end of religion, for the good of humanity we are forced to intervene. We cannot, however, take sides, as they are all my sons, although it may not appear that way.'

Using this divine pause, Fátima dared to give her opinion. 'And what about sending a plague down on JFK and Fidel Castro? Then an angel would appear to them and announce that it was a warning to learn to behave. What do you think?'

God listened to her wistfully, recalling the good old days when antibiotics had yet to be invented and everything was clear and simple. 'My dear, I see that you remain true to tradition, and this pleases me, but in modern times the old recipes no longer work. We have to be creative. To innovate.'

This craze for innovation left Fátima suspicious, convinced that change always brought something bad. 'Who am I to disagree?'

'So, no more about plagues, flus, or colds. We're going to use diplomacy.'

'Diplomacy?'

'Exactly, but this time we won't try and convince half the world. We just need these two to understand that peace is preferable to war.'

'I get it. You're going to offer them a place in heaven.'

'I can't. I would be found out straightaway and accused of cheating, but to be honest, it won't be easy for either of them to make it into heaven.'

'Look, tell me this: is it true that rich men can't enter heaven?'

'Oh, this is a parable, but in fact some can't get in.'

'Too right, too,' rejoiced Fátima, hitting her hand with her fist.

'Right, I'm going to send my son to knock some sense into them, and I need your help.'

Great joy filled Fátima's heart. She was sure that her worth would now be recognised and that she would play an important role. 'Are we to perform a miracle to dissuade them from violence?'

God listened to her, stupefied, and took his time to reply, convinced that this fashion had already passed. 'A miracle? Don't you know that miracles are old hat? Anyway, what miracle would you suggest?'

Illusions deflated, she floated back down to Earth without daring to count her dream of the Miracle of the Sun. After all, in pagan beliefs the sun played a very important role. Soaking up its rays in moderation gave a nice colour. Even oranges became sweeter, producing delicious marmalades. 'They had great miracles back in the old days,' she replied longingly, remembering incredible hauls of fish using nothing but basic methods, impossible cures without medicine, walking on water to save the shipwrecked, and even the very resuscitation of a dead man.

For a moment God felt the warm flavour of nostalgia of the good old days, too. Did he still have a parting of the waves in him? This had indeed been the most grandiose of his miracles, so grandiose and perfect that many still questioned its truthfulness. One thing was for sure. He would never again destroy a city, no matter how immoral the behaviour of its inhabitants. Architects, developers, and local authorities would never forgive him. He had acted on impulse, a thoughtless act that brought him notoriety for being revengeful and, as you can imagine, served little purpose for these incorrigible earthly sinners.

Well briefed on society's latest customs and trends, he countered: 'This was before. There were no television or films. Nowadays nobody is interested in miracles. They prefer to play the lottery, visit casinos, or rob banks.'

But Fátima, showing that sometimes it's easier for a camel to knit a woolly jumper than for mentalities to change, puffed up with courage and insisted, 'And what about a little eclipse?'

'A little eclipse?' God asked, caught off guard.

'Yes, like in that Tintin book.'

'You know full well that I don't have time to read comic books,' God exclaimed angrily.

Fátima tried to be convincing, putting as much charm as she could muster into her voice. 'An eclipse has the advantage of not being a miracle.'

'Obviously,' God chipped in, as a learned connoisseur of the mysteries of the universe.

'But the occlusion of the sun, the sudden darkness and

the drop in temperature arouse irrational feelings amongst people.'

'And then?'

'Then, anything can happen,' Fátima concluded, forgetting to complete her train of thought.

God, noticing the fragile nature of the plan and how the outcome of the intervention would be left to chance, joked, 'And what if they interpret the eclipse as nothing more than an eclipse?'

'That's where your son and I come into it.'

God tightened his grip on the handset. 'Would you like to tell me once and for all just what you intend?'

'When the moon passes over the sun, they will both be amazed, their mouths agape.'

'Yes, that's likely.'

'In that very moment we will appear and tell them that the end of the world is nigh.'

God became worried. 'And what if this makes them form a doomsday cult? What if they start knocking on doors and preaching misfortunes in my name?'

Fátima needed a few seconds to reply. 'It appears to me that the faith market is saturated; there isn't any room for more cults.'

'That's what you think. All it needs is for someone to preach some nonsense with great conviction and "ping!" suddenly they'll have followers hanging on their every word, taking everything they say as absolute truth.'

Fátima began to sweat, but remained firm in defence of her theory. 'Okay, if we have to, we'll threaten them with fire.'

God was shocked by the fundamentalism of his disciple. 'Hey, don't mention those blunders of the past. I'm entirely against such barbarian methods.'

'Me too, believe me. I just thought it might be a good idea to give them a fright,' Fátima maintained, while fiddling with a lighter.

'Don't play with fire, my child,' God rebuked her, imagining the scourge of forest fires.

'Of course, what I wanted to say was that under the effect of the eclipse they would both be vulnerable to our line of argument.'

God remained skeptical. 'I don't like this eclipse thing.'

Fátima wouldn't give up. 'Try and imagine this: the world becoming dark, JFK and Fidel petrified, your son and I suddenly appearing on a white horse.'

God put a damper on her enthusiasm: 'Fine, but my agreement with my son didn't say anything about an eclipse, and then who's going to put the moon in front of the sun?'

If the first observation left Fátima thoughtful, the second didn't even tweak her. 'Don't spare a thought about the sun and the moon. I've got it covered. As to your son, get him on the phone, please.'

'Just a second.' God laid the receiver to one side, asking the angels to tell Christ to come to the phone.

Moments later, the Saviour on the line, Fátima explained her daring plan once again, emphasising that she would be nothing more than a sidekick, with all the glory going his way. Christ listened to her without interrupting and, unlike his father, was fascinated by the story of the eclipse, imagining the dramatic effect of the phenomenon on the masses, his task made all the easier. Gradually they outlined an agreement. However, certain doubts still swirled in his mind, rankling him. What would be the right speech to best suit the circumstances? What words could dissolve the insensible hearts of the two warriors and be written in the sermon books of the future as a divine example of love among men? A chill passed through him at the thought of proffering innocuous phrases of the 'love each other, remain a virgin until you marry, don't covet your neighbour's wife' variety, and so on, thus failing in his mission. He felt another chill, this time more intensely, when he imagined the possibility of his new lessons on pacifism being considered inferior to those of Gandhi or to those of Mandela, who didn't even make it to demigods, and whose taste in clothing was horrendous, but who still managed to avoid much bloodshed.

He revealed his concerns to Fátima, who, very knowledgeable of human and divine psychology, decided to bolster the saviour's self-confidence, reminding him of the many times when he had demonstrated his ability to reason and had silenced his enemies: the doctors at the temple beaten in theological debate when he was just a child, the Sermon on the Mount and turning the other cheek, casting out the moneychangers from the temple (a little violent, it must be said), the lessons of humility given to rich men. Who had said to love your enemy before he did? Gandhi was a cheap imitation. Mandela was even worse. With such an impressive résumé, a doctorate in 'love for one another,' how could he fear the challenge?

Christ was used to being praised, his qualities lauded by bishops, priests, and nuns, but he had never been presented with such a eulogy. Much had been said and written about his life, all in agreement that he had humanised religion, had endeavoured to civilise mankind, and had given his life for them. But nothing resembled the portrait of him that Fátima was painting. Finally, someone had appeared who understood that his message was the origin of all positive changes undertaken by humanity.

The second coming of Christ was very different from the first, in that it occurred in another historical period, in that the age of the saviour was different, and that this time he didn't need to be born again, redoubling the confusion between believers about dogmas of virginity and metaphysical intercourse, and giving rise to humourous comments from atheists.

Other differences included the fact that Romans no longer ruled the known world, the Sanhedrin was dissolved, crucifixions had been abolished, prostitutes were no longer stoned in public; miracles had been considerably reduced following scientific advances; few understood that the drawing of a fish could mean anything other than a fish and of a dove, anything other than a dove; people now fled by plane instead of donkey, no rich man wanted to get rid of his assets without tax benefits; the price of treason was below thirty coins; plastic surgery had replaced transfiguration; Latin had given way to English; and people now considered cousins and siblings to be different from each other.

Similarities to be noted included the majority had identical resentment against men who wanted to change the established order; women continued to have more faith than men despite being excluded from religious functions; the many religions never agreed on the majority of metaphysical and political matters, despite being in agreement that sex is a great sin; using God's name to wage wars continued to be highly effective; tax collectors are hated; prodigal sons come back home when their money has run out; beautiful women are promised everything, the fashion of washing one's hands has stuck; predictions for the Apocalypse have stuck too; nobody wants to be called Cain or Jezebel; and there are plenty of people who turn water into wine.

This time Christ took steps and precautions so the same kind of failure didn't befall him as it did last time. He now had Fátima, an earthly contact, who would explain in detail the customs of these people, saving him a whole heap of misunderstandings and confusion. Furthermore, he wouldn't have to go around preaching to the masses, recruiting disciples, and defying authorities. He just had to avoid war and reconcile two estranged brothers. Now, just like before, he was left to his own devices and couldn't invoke his father's protection. This circumstance brought risks with it. For example, he could be poorly received by the two gentlemen and accused of being responsible for all the ills that plague mankind.

However, this new role of his, international conflict mediator, was beginning to please him. What's more, in this confusion between JFK and Fidel Castro, the reasons for the disagreement didn't lie in matters of faith, in the misuse of his name, as had been the case throughout the history of mankind. It involved nothing more than a war that a dictator had decided to start. Nevertheless, he had to keep in mind that the enemy of the dictator was a Christian. On the other hand, the dictator himself had been inspired by some of his teachings, although he resorted to practices that voided the theory. Seeing things in this light, the case now became much more complicated.

Fortunately he had Fátima as his assistant, this intelligent and insightful woman, who happened to be a great housewife too, who had come up with the brilliant idea of the solar eclipse as an antidote to war. It didn't bother him that sun eclipses had been exploited in former times by priests of pagan cults. But he had a slight doubt. What if Fátima couldn't do it? It was clear that he would have to shoulder the burden. But this was a prodigious miracle, which, being so out of practice, he was unsure he had the strength to perform.

Okay, he reasoned, she must be prepared to produce the phenomenon. Some humans have so-called supernatural powers. They can see into the future, cure the ill, find water under the ground, steal millions, and not go to prison.

Suddenly Christ was back walking on Earth – broad strides, graceful movements, shoulders back, hair waving in the wind, and a sparkle in his eye. His clothing, appropriate for a man of the people, made him unrecognisable. He found himself somewhere in the countryside, in a field planted with oak, chestnut, and olive trees, with a meandering stream at which animals were drinking.

In a slow separation, the sun bid farewell to the earth, apologising for leaving it with a wash of golden light in the treetops. Prudishly looking on, the sky's blue cheeks blushed orange. Inebriated by the sunset hues, birds floated on high. Christ stopped for a moment to admire the delights of nature, breathing in its aroma; his feeling of well-being knew no bounds. Then he fell to his knees, caressed the ground with both hands, and kissed it. In this caressing of the earth he experienced the warmth of the reunion with an ancient passion, as if he had never stopped loving. He was unable to contain his emotion and let fall a tear. In that moment, he was no more than a man.

How different it was to look down on the Earth from up there, so far away where it was so cold, to feeling it down here where it could be savoured with every sense. Men yearn for paradise, but lost in fanciful daydreams about an Eden made of fantasy, they rarely see it when it passes by. The heavenly garden from which he had come was nothing in comparison to this stunning nature that he found unchanged. Maybe the beings from there didn't need to kill to survive or to die so that others lived. Maybe eternal security had no price. It was certain the people from here were condemned to the laws of survival, were constantly accompanied by fear throughout their existence, but how could you compare the sterile home of some with the splendid place of others?

He suddenly understood the pantheists, worshippers of a physical world as a divine manifestation. His father had done an amazing job, only within the reach of a god. He might have done it in seven days, but he must have taken millennia to think it up. It's hard to imagine that something this beautiful could exist in the universe. The water, the earth, the light, the fascination of permanent change, so many different living beings, the excrement of a cow nourishing a flower. He almost dared to think the only species that wasn't needed was the human.

This blasphemous idea, especially for him, as he had been human and had even had two fathers, had now haunted him more than once.

Everything was fine, a wondrous work achieved, so why did his father have to pick up his brush and add two more characters to the painting? It seemed to him that the painting had been ruined. The idea of creating beings in his image and likeness was good and original. But, as the Progenitor himself would have admitted, the result fell well short of expectations.

It began badly from the outset when his father decided to place the two nudes (they could have at least worn underwear, for God's sake) in a garden with apple trees and snakes, decreeing that they were not permitted to eat the fruit. God should have known that this could only lead to nonsense. Of course, it was only a matter of time before they would be biting into that apple. And you couldn't blame the snake because these were two grownups who knew right from wrong. Snakes are innocent and good remedies can be made from their venom, expensive handbags and shoes from their skin. So, worried about the other temptations such weak and sinful flesh would succumb to, muscular angels chased Adam and Eve away. We all know the disaster that ensued. Once expelled from paradise they multiplied, committed crimes in the family, organised armies, and went out to enter into warfare over water, over wheat, over gold, over diamonds, and oil. Any pretext served them to massacre each other. And to put an end to this unending tragedy, the war between JFK and Fidel Castro.

Fortunately, these two counsellors had a guardian angel watching over them who was well connected in heaven. And here he was again, with different experience, back with his blundering brothers to try and reconcile them.

Fátima didn't turn up at the place where they had agreed to meet. Christ searched and searched. 'Yoo-hoo, Fátima,' he called, but there was no sign of her.

Maybe she was on the other side of the stream. Of course, she'd never lift her skirt or get her shoes wet to cross it. He walked across the water, not realising what he had done until he reached the other side. He had promised his father that he wouldn't resort to magic power or perform miracles for no good reason, and he feared he might be caught. But neither Fátima nor anyone else was there to see him. Where on earth could she be?

Fátima knew she was running late, but she couldn't resist

watching the last episode of the Mexican soap opera *Besame Mucho*. How could she ever sleep without knowing whether Rosita would marry Paco, if the rogue Roberto would be punished for his actions, and who would take care of little Joselito? Of course she and Christ were meeting about a serious matter, but he, an example of patience and tolerance, would certainly understand her reasons.

With Rosita and Paco in the church and Joselito, the ring bearer, and Roberto, the sly rogue, in jail, the soap had ended well. She fetched her donkey and galloped off to meet the saviour.

Taking a shortcut, she headed down a track pocked with potholes, causing her back pain each time the donkey stepped into one of them. As she approached her destination, analysis of the soap opera gave way to examining the motives behind her being on a donkey at that time of day at such speed.

War had been a fact of life since men settled on the earth and created wealth, and no civilisation had been able to deny it, but there had always been figures who opposed violence, sometimes managing, when not taken prisoner or beheaded, to return good sense to the barbarians. Their fearless actions had saved the lives of millions of human beings. Now it was her turn. The huge responsibility of stopping JFK and Fidel Castro from bringing a new disaster to earth lay in her hands. The task was titanic. Both were stubborn and pigheaded, and war means good business. She felt like Atlas, carrying the world on her shoulders, a column with an entablature on her head. What left her distraught was the burden imposed by having to produce the eclipse. She had made this suggestion in the heat of the telephone conversation, but she now feared she had acted rashly. All things considered, she knew nothing about eclipses, astronomy, or astrology, nor had she until then produced a miracle, however simple. She was great at cooking, and ironed like no one, but those skills were not enough.

Suddenly the sun penetrated a cloud with a rosy light, and it seemed like a good omen. After all, if Rosita had married

Paco, why couldn't JFK and Castro bury the hatchet?

In the meantime, Christ had sat down under a tree, closed his eyes, and begun to think about how he should proceed, the right words to use, the tone of voice, and the appropriate gestures.

Nevertheless, he prepared himself for the worst-case scenario. What if, as happened last time, the majority of the people, or even all of them, didn't recognise him? What if, after introducing himself, 'Dearest brethren, I am Christ, and I have come to put an end to this war,' he was received with the response, 'This guy is a nutter,' or worse, assaulted and arrested? What would he do? As he couldn't perform any miracles, he would have to resort to his powers of reasoning to dissuade them from violence, as he had done in the past with those who wanted to stone Maria Magdalena.

The phrase 'Make love, not war' jumped into his head. *A great phrase*, he thought, as the word 'love' was understood in its full meaning, that of brotherhood and tolerance among men, marriage for life, and peaceful coexistence with the in-laws. Ninety percent spirit and the rest for the flesh. All the same, what if they decided to interpret the phrase in the modern way, and this led to a new sexual revolution, with orgies on every corner? No, this idea of 'making love' was too dangerous. In fact, the concept of love between human beings was an extremely complicated thing and the matter of ongoing contention. For some, those considered virtuous, it was the highest form of union between a man and a woman, but they understood the need for a religious matrimony. For others, those labelled as sinners, monogamy was out of the question. For others still, the most complicated of all, true love could only happen with someone of the same sex.

It was obvious that there was no single norm. Banning things was of little use, and to make matters worse, many of those who preached morals weren't exactly the best examples.

These reflections were interrupted by the distant sound of Fátima's donkey's hooves, and Christ saw a woman riding his way.

The meeting between the saviour and his most loyal disciple began very respectfully. Fátima curtseyed, and Christ did the same. Then, before moving onto the topic at hand, they discussed trivial matters. They enquired as to each other's health, and Fátima praised his resistance to ageing.

As night was fast approaching, with stars lighting up the sky, Fátima suggested they set off for her house, the reception venue tacitly agreed upon during telephone negotiations. The animal was exhausted, so they both walked on foot to save the quadruped a cruel effort that would have certainly been denounced by any animal welfare association.

Just as they prepared to start discussing the right strategy for intervening in the conflict, they passed some peasants riding in an oxcart and heard the following comment: 'Look at those two. They have a donkey and walk on foot,' followed by coarse laughter. Christ and Fátima acknowledged the rural provocation and looked at each other without knowing what to do. Finally Fátima suggested that he should ride on the animal. Christ looked at the beast to check whether it would be able to take his weight. Seriously doubting that it would, but not wanting to offend his hostess, he did as she said. As the donkey did not protest – after all, it's not every day that you get to carry the son of God – he forgot the incident and started the conversation again, asking Fátima if she knew the probable site where the two armies would meet. Fátima replied that rumour had it that JFK was on a hill close to her village where he was preparing a trap for Fidel Castro.

Accustomed to traps, Christ asked if there was a traitor in the Castro ranks – someone who would tell Fidel to go to a place on his own, a garden for example, where enemy forces would be waiting to capture him. Fátima admitted that she knew of no stratagem that JFK was planning to use, adding only that there was talk of digging holes. Christ immediately understood the ruse, but he saw no need to explain how it worked. However, he couldn't help but imagine falling into a pit of sharpened stakes, an image that brought unpleasant memories to mind, causing him to think that men were really cruel. His father had been right; something had gone wrong with these unpredictable creatures.

As they entered the outskirts of her village, they passed by a house where an elderly woman and a cat were at the window. Seeing Christ and Fátima, the woman was unable to contain her feminist thoughts. 'Good God', she yelled out the window. 'That lazy good-for-nothing rides a donkey while the poor lady has to walk!' Once again a feeling of embarrassment crept up between them. This time, Christ felt he should take an attitude that would silence once and for all these people so given to voicing their opinion on things that didn't concern them. So he climbed off the donkey and invited Fátima to take his place.

Christ resumed their dialogue by asking her how she was going to create the eclipse. Not knowing what to reply, Fátima ducked the question, implying that it was going to be a surprise, and added that the eclipse was only the ideal scenario for the new apparition of the saviour, with the true solution to avoiding the war lying in his wise words. This flattering line of argument did not leave Christ indifferent, but it did not remove his doubts as to the ability of his disciple to perform the astronomic phenomenon. Even so, he didn't persist, feeling increasingly confident that he alone would be able to solve any problem.

The warm twilight had invited squadrons of mosquitoes to set out from their bases, intent on stinging attacks. Nevertheless, whether through superior interference or through some strange instinct stopping them from sucking the divine blood of Christ, they only bit Fátima and the donkey.

The sufferers were defending themselves from the vampire fury of the insects as they entered the village. A group of drunkards commented, 'You can see who wears the trousers in that household.' As Christ was above any provocation – sticks and stones could break his bones, but words would never hurt him – he ignored the insult without needing to turn the other cheek. However, Fátima, fearing she was the cause of a grave affront to the saviour, immediately got down from her mount, and the two ended their journey walking alongside the donkey.

Fátima lived in a modest little house made of local stone that was topped with a straw roof. The donkey's stall stood to the side, together with a chicken coop and a vegetable garden. And it was thus, in this modest rural property, that Christ found shelter for his second coming to earth.

Once through the wooden gate that she never locked, Fátima took the animal, truly deserving of rest, to its stall, asking Christ to wait a moment. As he waited, he was moved to be met with such a pure and welcoming place, the antithesis of ancient and modern Babylonia, safe from the invasion of mass culture, and from the cultureless masses, in which men lived in harmony with nature and where time and money never mixed. Touched, he couldn't help but reflect once again on the expulsion of Adam and Eve from paradise, daring to speculate that if they had lived in a place like this, no matter how many snakes and apple trees in the backyard, even naked and willing to experience new things, it would all have been so different. The path of humanity would have gone another direction war would never have existed, and Fidel Castro and JFK would have been the best of friends.

Fátima then returned, opened the front door, lit an oil lamp, and invited him to enter the house. She didn't say, 'Make yourself at home,' nor did she say, 'Make yourself comfortable; take off your shoes.' She simply proceeded in a manner similar to which she had since meeting with Christ, words of courtesy replaced by the joyous expression on her face and the graceful gesture she made to show him the sofa.

Comfortably seated while his hostess checked the pans left on the stove, Christ returned his thoughts to original sin. Adam and Eve sharing domestic chores, he scrubbing the floor and she roasting prime rib, peeling potatoes, and plucking a chicken. Later, the pair set the table, savouring the produce of the earth. 'You cook so well, my dear,' he'd say. 'Only to please you, my love,' she'd say. Then they would sit hand in hand on the sofa, so in love, they would be happy their whole lives long and have plenty of children without the trace of a thought of sinning so feeble-mindedly.

While Christ was thinking about the story of Adam and Eve, Fátima placed two steaming bowls of vegetable soup onto the table and offered him a seat at the head. He sat down for his first supper since the last. This time he felt relaxed as he didn't need to share the meal with twelve other guests nor proffer revelations on treachery committed by someone present. It was only when he placed a spoonful in his mouth and felt the delicious cabbage dissolve on his palate that he realised he was ravenous. He then asked permission, cut himself a large chunk of cornbread, and settled down to his soup without another word.

To follow, accompanied by wine, Fátima served a black pudding risotto, the blood-soaked appearance of which, at first, left Christ suspicious. His gastronomic misgivings were short-lived though, and he was unable to contain his pleasure. 'Mmmm, delicious,' he said with the first taste of sausage, much to the delight of the cook, who proudly confided the origin of her grandmother's old recipe to him.

And once again he returned to the controversy of the expulsion from paradise, hypothesising that if the forbidden fruit had been black pudding risotto instead of the apple, then surely nobody would have been able to resist it. In this light, you could even understand their inability to remove the temptation from their minds. He himself would have to call on all his strength not to eat it. But give into apples? Apple sauce, maybe, but otherwise it was difficult for him to understand. Obviously, these ramblings went completely unnoticed by Fátima, who was supposedly able to create an eclipse but apparently unable to guess the thoughts of others.

They took coffee and brandy on the sofa after Fátima had cleared the table, ignoring Christ's offers to help. 'Guests do not work in my house,' she said. They were sitting at either end of the sofa when the hostess got up, exclaiming, 'Now it's time for your surprise!' From below a broken floorboard, she pulled out a wooden box. Then, smiling enigmatically, she opened it and held it out to Christ as if it were a gift of incense or myrrh. 'Try one; they're incredible.'

Surprised, Christ could smell the warm aroma of the plump cylinders and took one, eyeing it curiously. The red band read *Cohiba Siglo XXI*. A true connoisseur, Fátima explained that they were cigars from Fidel's country that you could buy at good prices at fairs authorised by JFK. 'They're at war, yet still trade goods?' Christ asked, perplexed. Fátima took a cigar, removed the band, cut off the tip with a knife, and lit it. After two puffs of smoke savoured in sinful lust, she found the most appropriate answer, 'Is it the cigar's fault?'

The Saviour was a little disappointed, but, understanding human weaknesses and urged by Fátima to try such magnificent cigars, he ended up lighting his. After all, he was immune to all those terrible threats appearing on cigarette packs, his lungs so pure with celestial air. But the experience wasn't a good one for him. His attempt at inhaling the smoke resulted in a violent coughing fit which even Fátima's slaps on the back couldn't put an end to.

A little later, Fátima picked up her sewing basket, threaded a needle, and started to darn some socks. There to work, Christ looked inside the basket, chose a red pair, and with the skill of an experienced seamstress began to sew up the holes in the heels too. But after fifteen minutes, fatigue took hold of the workers, forcing them to interrupt their job.

After letting out a yawn, Fátima had to acknowledge that she was exhausted and suggested to Christ that they retire for the evening, offering him her room, saying she would sleep on the sofa. Christ smiled at his hostess's hospitality, but said he couldn't possibly accept.

When he was left alone in the room, he got up and went outdoors. Outside, with the crickets chirruping, he contemplated the immensity of the sky, the smallness of the stars, and the sliver of moon. Seen from Earth, the universe seemed even larger to him, infinite. Amazed at the celestial spectacle, he was reminded of a book he had once read called *Cosmos*, in which it was said that everything in existence was made of the same material, whether a man or a galaxy. Had JFK and Fidel Castro ever wondered about this beautiful yet baffling truth? Could hatred exist in the heart of anyone meditating on the subject? A sudden bout of homesickness led him to wave up to his father, the architect of harmony and chaos, who was no doubt looking at him that very moment. He then walked over to the donkey's stable, lay down in the soft straw, and fell asleep, warmed by the hot breath of the animal.

That night, Christ had a dream: Adam and Eve were in paradise, but they were not enjoying the delights of happiness. Instead, they seemed deeply agitated, running about the gardens looking for something that Christ was unable to understand. Their heads moved from side to side as they tried to reveal any threat, their faces expressing the fear they were desperately trying to control. They were holding hands and moving very quickly, crouching down, sometimes hiding behind trees or lying on the ground in an attempt to hide from someone only they could see. The feeling they experienced was close to terror, but they were impelled by a powerful desire to confront the invisible threat. Eve displayed great courage, encouraging Adam, who seemed insecure. 'We can do it, we can do it' she said. When they came across a forest, they let go of each other's hands and ran as quickly as they could, storming into the dense tree cover, sensing that they were very close. (Christ jerked his legs in his sleep as if he himself were moving at great speed, waving his arms to avoid hitting the branches.) They were out of breath and their hearts thumped in their chests. They were running faster than humanly possible through the forest, which seemed as if it would never end, an inescapable conveyor belt of trees. Their progress was measured by the crunch of leaves crushed under their bare feet, their eyes glazed over in panic, like animals pursued by a predator.

Then, suddenly, they found a gap in the trees, placing them at the edge of paradise. Nothing but a red line was traced in the ground. With no barrier or fence, it seemed there was nothing to stop them from crossing. Adam and Eve stood there, trembling before the vision of their dreams, but, so close to salvation, they were unable to move, paralysed by the horror of committing the deadly sin. (Christ hoped fervently that they would escape.) A flying serpent then appeared, encouraging them to flee from paradise, promising wonders on the other side, flicking a forked tongue. Adam and Eve, tempted as they were, seemed ready to move forward. The dream seemed to linger at that moment until guards burst out from nowhere, pointing guns at them and leading them back to the Lord in paradise to be sentenced for having tried to escape. Then suddenly, Fidel Castro appeared, imposing and furious. Hurling terrifying invectives at them for their ungratefulness, he condemned them to death, before the mocking laughter of the winged demon.

Christ awoke when light pierced through the cracks in the stable. Memory of the dream came to him in blurred, out-of-order sequences. He tried to reorder the fragments to find meaning. He remained thus, trying to understand the bizarre association between paradise, the snake, the desire of the parents of humanity to escape, and Fidel Castro, until his empty stomach rescued his dream interpretation reverie. He got up, stroked the donkey, whose dreams had been much less complex, and, with toast and milky coffee on his mind, opened the wooden door. Fátima, an early riser, was already in the backyard watering the vegetables. She showed no surprise seeing him come out of the stable.

After satisfying his hunger, Christ had the idea of practising the eclipse, to test Fátima's abilities. He wondered if she would take offence at such a display of disbelief in her abilities. He would have to proceed with tact and diplomacy. In an angelic voice, he tried to show her that prudence advised that she at least attempt a test run of the eclipse. If his own father had done the same with Adam and Eve, humanity would be much more evolved, and this war would never have existed.

Fátima listened to him carefully. She had an inkling that Christ might not have faith in her powers. Convincing herself this was the case, for a moment she doubted her ability to eclipse the sun too, but in the end she ended up agreeing with the suggestion of a practice run, understanding that it would be a good test of her powers.

Rosita would have done the same.

So they decided to climb the nearby mountain, which seemed the most suitable place for such an experiment. This time they left the donkey behind, to avoid comments that might spoil their concentration. The climb was more difficult than they had imagined. The task forced them to test their human and divine motor skills for more than an hour.

Used to more elevated perspectives, the stunning panorama left Christ amazed as he contemplated the forests, the plains, and the watercourses that formed the spirit of the place, known in other times and other languages as *genius loci*. Kept entertained by their observations, or perhaps trying to build up the courage to move on to the eclipse test, they let time pass by as they talked at length on the wonders of local nature.

At midday, the sun's zenith reminded them why they were there and the task they were supposed to carry out. 'Perhaps we'd better start,' Christ said.

'I'm ready,' Fátima replied. Then, resembling followers of pagan gods who had climbed the mountain to worship the sun, Christ and Fátima got ready to start the eclipse experiment.

Fátima moved a few steps away from Christ and stared at the blue sky. She pulled out her mirrored sunglasses and put them on, forcing the saviour to stifle a fit of giggles, and quickly glanced up at the star she intended to momentarily snuff out.

Then, a little stunned by the direct impact of the solar glare, she placed her fingertips on her temples, deepened her breathing, tried to relax her muscles, and began to telepathically order the sun to dim its brightness down to absolute darkness. Christ was once again forced to stifle a torrent of guffaws. Fátima remained in this position of ultimate concentration for more than fifteen minutes, her face becoming redder and redder.

Meanwhile, nothing happened. The sun continued to shine, bursting with light throughout Fátima's test. Finally, worn out and irritated, she gave up, allowing her arms to fall, dropping any hopes of achieving an eclipse through telepathic means. Seeing that she was defeated and on the verge of fainting, Christ tried to comfort her.

'Don't be hard on yourself; these things can happen.'

'I really tried, but I just can't put it out.'

This reply left Christ perplexed. 'Put it out?'

'Yes.'

'Ah, I see. You were just approaching this from the wrong angle. You don't need to put the sun out. What you must do is place the moon between the sun and the earth.'

Fátima felt irritated at her display of ignorance. 'You mean I have to move the moon, then?'

'Exactly.'

'Nobody's up there at the moment exploring it, are they?'

'No, now they want to go to Mars.'

A new attempt followed, this time with the moon as her target, since the sun, a very large and hot nuclear reactor, wasn't something you could just turn on or off at a whim, as if it were some kind of lamp. The moon, however, was much smaller, much closer, its rotation matching the Earth's revolution around the sun. It always faced the same direction, it didn't follow the laws of gravity, and it influenced tides, menstrual cycles, and insanity. It had already been walked on and explored, had given great steps for mankind without any visible consequences, and it looked like a hole-pocked ball of

Swiss cheese.

Nevertheless, an unexpected obstacle was blocking the path of Fátima's wishes: neither of them could locate the moon. Some days nothing seems to go right.

'Where's it gone to?' Fátima wondered aloud.

'I can't see it anywhere either.'

Both were looking for it in the vast sky, forgetting the inflexible rules of its elliptical movement around the earth, when Christ came up with a solution for the impasse. 'It probably makes no difference whether we can see it or not. We'll give it a go anyway.' Fátima took off her sunglasses, bit her bottom lip, passed her hands through her hair, and turned her toes from side to side, but she didn't dare refuse the challenge.

Although she chose to use her mental powers to move the moon, the method of telepathy was replaced by that of telekinesis, which basically involves moving objects with thoughts alone.

To produce a lunar telekinesis, Fátima once again moved a few metres away and sat down, crossing her legs like a yoga master. Shifting her position to relieve the discomfort of a pointed stone in her behind, she then placed her hands on her knees. Then, without giving any order to the moon, she concentrated so that it would move to place itself in the exact position between the sun and the earth. This time she felt she wasn't going to fail. The moon was female after all, unlike the masculine, macho sun. And in her mind she could already see this cosmic carousel in which a bold satellite dared to interrupt the luminous relationship between a star and a planet, casting darkness over the earth and its inhabitants.

But no matter how much she tried, nothing happened. The moon didn't cover the sun. In a last ditch attempt, Fátima gritted her teeth and focused all her strength on controlling the movement of lunar revolution. A few moments went by and nothing changed. Desperate, she redoubled her concentration, clenched her fists and tensed up all over, and suddenly, *Bam!*

Just for fun, Christ decided to make a suggestion. 'Hey, what if you started to chant like those Tibetan monks who shave their heads and wrap up in orange cloths?' So Fátima began to moan 'Mmmmm' and more 'Mmmmm' and more 'Mmmmm,' until, fed up with the racket and with his fingers in his ears, Christ could contain himself no longer: 'Enough. That'll do for today.'

Fátima opened her eyes and looked at him in surprise. Scientific experiments needed time and patience. How many years did Galileo spend looking at the moon through a telescope, making calculations, enduring judgments and threats of fire to conclude that the Earth is always moving. And so, when Christ was getting ready to start the descent back to the house, she requested five more minutes, to make a last attempt at bringing about the eclipse. Inspired this time by films and cartoons. Seeing her so anxious to carry out the final tests, he was unable to say no.

With the failure of the telepathic and telekinetic methods, Fátima decided to try the magic ritual of the rain dance, but change it up a bit into a moon dance. Therefore, before launching into her lunar dance, she began some warm-up exercises, rotating her neck, waist, and wrists, flexing her knees, and attempting to touch her toes.

Then she began her moon dance, revealing choreography not dissimilar to that of cheerleaders, to which she added a few fitness exercises, forgetting that she was in the middle of an experiment to eclipse the light of the sun. It resulted, nevertheless, in a relaxed and graceful posture, as you would see in an adolescent in a nightclub. It caught Christ's attention, but that could possibly be due to the dust she had kicked up. However, for this reason, or for any other reason that can be explained by the laws of physics, the moon did not change its trajectory, and the sun continued to light up the earth.

In short, the failure was complete.

Fidel Castro's forces left at dawn, leaving the town in the hands of its inhabitants, who were unyielding to the Castro revolution or any other attempt to change their customs or transform their mentalities. For this reason, with the exception of the withdrawal of the invaders, day-to-day life in the town didn't change, since El Comandante, warned by the riot caused by the first and last debriefing session, decided to suspend revolutionary reforms indefinitely. Paradoxically, collective participation in this session proved the only revolutionary influence retained by the townsfolk. And they met once again in the same place to decide if they should free the priest and Lola or keep them detained. The whole thing proved very civil, with the majority choosing to free them both.

The two prisoners remained silent and cautious during this people's trial, without daring to utter a word in their own defence. When at last they were set free, they left through the crowd without looking at anyone, packed up their belongings, and left town. Watching their backs as they left, the people felt dismayed, a lump in their throats, with the sensation of having committed an injustice. And so, forced by wounded dignity into exile, the priest and Lola, guilty of nothing but wanting the best for the people, became, after the invasion (before the invasion it had been Varadero), the first victims of the tragedy of Fidel Castro.

Arranged into a square formation   modelled by revolutionary discipline, Castro's troops advanced through enemy territory without meeting any resistance. To the front, on foot, the infantry; behind, on horseback, Fidel and his commandants; in the middle, tied and gagged, in a cart pulled by a donkey, Varadero. The military precision of the soldiers did not come from the desire to serve a cause or from blind faith in an ideal. It arose out of the fear of punishment and, more disturbing still, of disrespecting the supreme authority they had been taught to idolise. Sons and grandsons of those who had felt the terror of the former regime and, with Fidel at their sides, had overthrown it. They knew the origin of the revolution from books, from teachers' lectures, and from endless speeches made by El Comandante. The repression of the previous dictator, the revolutionary euphoria, and the period of improvement to living standards represented an abstraction to them. It was something like a fairytale about a wicked witch.

When they became politically aware, the new regime, exalted by propaganda, was dying, while the previous one, classified as an abomination, seemed as if it had never existed. During the 'Special Period,'[8] which in practice had not yet ended, they felt deprivation and hunger, the betrayal of dreams, despair, and inability to believe in the future. They all had great scientific, literary, and artistic skills, which served no purpose. Sitting on the wall separating the island from the sea, they watched on in fury as tourists took their women. A rebellion was expanding within them, and the reason for their misfortune was called Fidel Castro.

Nevertheless, the commandants could still remember what life was like under Fulgencio Batista. They were proud of having fought him and having been part of building a new society. As a result they were unable to revolt against Fidel and hence deny their own past. If their belief in the revolution had also faded, their honour and dignity remained intact. For them, the constant memory of the past, surrounding themselves with old photos, repeating stories that were almost true, in which they were almost heroes, allowed them, for the moment, to put up with the present. The majority also wanted change, but preferred to let providence undertake this mission.

The army was heading toward the northeast, avoiding obstacles in the terrain, and the narrowest passes, which were

---

8. *Período especial*, the Special Period, refers to the economic crisis in Cuba in 1991. With the dissolution of the Soviet Union, trade with the socialist bloc diminished.

prone to ambushes. Not a sign could be found of the enemy. In the meantime, the march of the Castro forces seemed more like a stroll in the country. The novelty of the vegetation and the geological formations diverted the attention of the soldiers from any thoughts of death. Contemplating this uncharted world, which became greener and greener the more they moved away from the south, the call to sedition lessened.

With Varadero silenced, Fidel regained the fighting spirit of former battles and the ability to guide men into war. Even those who hated him most, those who desperately wished death upon him, became models of military obedience, their ideas of revolt withering in his mere presence. Fidel was aware of this, and strived for direct contact with the soldiers during moments of rest. Seeing him so close, the soldiers, still flesh and bone, were petrified that some physiognomic sign might unveil the conspiracies they were silently plotting. It was at times like these, when he could feel the spell of his charisma, that he understood the price he had paid for the fear of being assassinated – losing contact with the people – had maybe been greater than death itself.

During the night, flaming tongues leapt from the logs of the campfires. The voices of groups of men sitting around the fires blended in an incomprehensible soup of whispers and moans. Prayers learned in childhood were repeated, the meaning of which the men had never fully grasped, transforming them now into entreaties begging, without ever naming him, for the death of Fidel Castro.

When everyone, apart from the sentry guards and Fidel, was sleeping the deep sleep of bodies worn out by fatigue, an unexpected event took place. Emerging from the darkness, dragging wisps of mist, a masked horseman approached the camp, dismounted when asked to stop by the guards, and declared he had important information. After forcing him to uncover his face, the soldiers frisked him and tried in vain to question him. 'Who are you? What are you doing here?'

His only reply, even when treated to rifle-butt blows and kicks, was that he would only talk to Fidel Castro. The temerity of the stranger, and the conviction with which he guaranteed that he had a secret that would decide the final battle against JFK, intimidated the soldiers. Meanwhile, the horseman, sensing the guards' disarray and appearing more accustomed to giving orders than obeying them, began to shout at them with authority, 'I demand to be brought before Fidel Castro,' reversing the initial balance of power.

The impasse came to an end with El Comandante's arrival. Impeccably groomed in his camouflage fatigues, khaki cap, and brown boots, he was confronted with a stranger dressed in black who, finger pointed skyward, was ranting at the sentries like a guard in a labour camp. Surprised, he stopped in front of the group, enjoying the scene before him. Despite having their backs to him, the soldiers, their strings strummed by the energy emanating from Fidel, could feel a vibration and, guessing at his presence, immediately lined up.

It was only then that the horseman realised that someone had arrived and prudently became silent. Fidel watched the man with wildly gleaming eyes, curious about the adventurer who was risking his life to talk to him. A strange empathy was kindled within him as he understood that he was before a leader. He may have been an enemy, someone who wanted to kill him, perhaps a traitor devoid of scruples, but Fidel could sense that he had found someone who was capable of imposing his will on others. Few challenges stimulated Fidel as much as measuring the strength of a man who felt worthy to face up to him in a game of strategy and nerves, which few adversaries were allowed to play, and in which he had never been beaten. Military success gave him great pleasure, but nothing compared to bending a recalcitrant spirit, to submit someone to his will.

'Identify yourself and tell us your purpose here!'

'I am J.E. Hoover. I bring information concerning JFK.'

Sitting at a table inside El Comandante's tent, J.E. Hoover and Fidel Castro began to enjoy a cigar tempered by a glass of *añejo* rum before starting their conversation. Given that whenever you want something from someone you should try to please them, Fidel offered him the best in his possession. The cigar did not surprise the visitor, who was used to receiving similar gifts from smugglers, but the rum, from secret blends available only to the revolutionary elite, left him delighted. When the tobacco smoke had permeated the tent with a perfumed mist, and the warming energy of the drink spread from their stomachs to the rest of their bodies, the conditions had been created for them both to begin the tough negotiations.

Fidel urged J. E. Hoover to open the game. 'What do you have to offer me?'

'You shouldn't attack JFK. He has set up a trap that will decimate your soldiers,' he replied, before entering into a long explanation of the pit system: its location, the number of pits, and the terrible consequences they would produce. He described in morbid detail the torture of those who did not die immediately, and then launched into information about the number of men the president had and the strategy he was going to take. As J. E. Hoover spoke, he relished his own words, savouring them as he had the rum. As was the case during meetings with JFK, he believed that his voice would be listened to, this time by the great Fidel Castro, who, in a reverential silence, received his advice. Assured of his importance, he mused on great battles of the past in which cunning, not force, had won the day. Then he praised the strategy and the revolutionary triumph of El Comandante.

While he listened, Fidel began to make a mental sketch of the character talking endlessly in front of him. His initial stroke seemed to reveal strength, the second boldness and fearlessness, and in the following strokes, cunning, ingenuity, and pragmatism. Nevertheless, a thick line covered the previous sketches, shaping the betrayal. All the same, although he despised him, as he did all renegades, he recognised that he was in possession of the trump for conquering JFK. But if it had proven easy to reveal the soul of this man, what interested him now were the reasons behind his desertion. 'Why did you come to me? What are you hoping to gain from this?'

Having arrived at the point where his fortune or misfortune were at stake, J. E. Hoover, aware that confessing his true motive – a lack of faith in the future of his country – would prove catastrophic in trivialising the betrayal, and that a simulated conversion to the ideals of the revolution would be laughable – he even feared unleashing a fit of giggles if he proclaimed the wish for equality amongst men – he plumped for the role of hero, rebelling against the injustices of JFK. He believed that in doing so he would touch Fidel's sensitive side. So, he began to tell how JFK had increased taxes, expelled the peasants from the land, tolerated corruption, and, finally, suppressed the grievances of the people. He had protested against such royal outrages, which had led to him being persecuted and forced to flee to avoid prison. And why did he do this? What did he want? Nothing! The interests moving him were not material. He just wanted to continue to serve the state by ensuring common security in fighting the enemies that conspired against it, a role performed with irreprehensible zeal as any capable citizen would testify.

Suddenly, Fidel, who up till that point had been listening suspiciously to J. E. Hoover's story – he never believed anyone entirely and worked from the principle that every truth held a lie – discovered in him some use and began to look at him almost affectionately. Nevertheless, despite already knowing about the trap JFK was preparing for him, something crucial was missing for him to feel entirely satisfied with the conversation, as if the dialogue were nothing more than a prelude to the final moment of glory. Until now he had let Hoover talk, creating the illusion that he believed him to be useful and accepted his services. The moment had arrived to subdue him. To begin, Fidel almost begged his forgiveness for the violence of the guards and for the modesty of the rooms in which he received him. Then he spoke about the responsibility of those who look for the common good. But, in the end, with no concern for originality, he alluded to sinking ships, to shipwrecks, and to rats that rush to escape disaster.

J. E. Hoover had been getting ready to present a plan for the annihilation of Fidel's enemies, when these words sucked the air out of his lungs. Suffocating, he suddenly understood that El Comandante, besides despising him, considered him of no use. The dream of being the eye and ear of the Castro powerhouse vanished before it had even started. He had assessed his importance badly and had presupposed that the rules of political play were the same whatever the regime. Yet, on the Castro chessboard, with Fidel as king, all other pieces were dispensable. So, he had voluntarily moved from being the invulnerable queen of JFK to being Fidel Castro's pawn, ready to be sacrificed. If he were able to escape from the other game, he would never leave this one. Tied to the ropes of his fears, not knowing which square to move to, seeing himself in the position in which he had so often placed others, he couldn't manage another word. He then heard Fidel's triumphant words: 'You shouldn't have come!'

That night, not far from Varadero, J. E. Hoover recalled his escape from the camp of JFK, hours after having assured him that God was on his side and that Fidel Castro would be crushed. Ever since the last meeting, he had begun to think about deserting. He doubted the ability of the elite to find ways of progress and was certain that the only thing that really interested the people was football. In recent times, signs of moral and ethical degradation had multiplied. He discovered that nobody followed the law, theft had spiralled out of control, incompetent people held very important positions of power, and public places – from schools to sports arenas – were infested with savages. Before such a dark picture, a harbinger of imminent doom, he could see no possible solution. The problem did not lie in lack of education, or in contempt for knowledge, or the numbing caused by television. The reason was atavistic; a received and transmitted illness. The country was stubbornly walking toward the abyss and now nothing could stop it. Who could blame him for being more clairvoyant than anyone else and for defending his interests?

All the same, believing himself to be the right man for Fidel Castro's dictatorship, he discovered he was insignificant. In truth, he had only believed in luck, in chance, in off-the-cuff strategies. Yes, he too had been unable to avoid the disease eating away at the nation. He thought he was above the people, but he was basically made from the exact same stuff.

With great composure and peace of mind, J. E. Hoover lifted the stone from one of his emblazoned rings and swallowed the sweet powder hidden therein.

In the meantime, Fidel was digesting the information he had received, trying to fit it into reasoning that supported the invasion. The knowledge of JFK's trap allowed him to escape an embarrassing defeat, which would have put him in the hall of fame for mediocre strategists shamed forever throughout history. On the other hand, his enemy, taking into account the flight of the traitor Hoover, would be forced to change his original strategy to create a new plan at very short notice. Projecting his own fears onto the enemy perhaps, he was in no doubt, therefore, that a feeling of great tension hung over JFK's army. The desertion of J. E. Hoover had weakened the opponent forces.

With the possibility of suffering an ignominious defeat removed, he could focus on the main issue: what advantages would victory bring him? To conquer whomever propaganda had transformed into the person guilty of every, misfortune, and displaying prisoners of war in a triumphal parade, would incite great joy in the people. This was the objective. The trick would work, of this he was certain, but since this was just palliative care and not the remedy for the illness – as there was no cure – how long would its effects last? Wouldn't the protests return within a few months and would it be necessary, in an endless vicious circle, to invent a new enemy, to transform it into a new source for every evil and, once again, begin another war? As such, winning would do him little good. The solution lay elsewhere. After a fierce battle, the landscape stained with blood, strewn with corpses, the sky swarming with vultures, he would have to be defeated and die like a martyr. Alive he was condemned to shame; in death he could aspire to posthumous glory.

Simple as that.

After all, Che Guevara had become a legend because he had died. He had become a symbol of the struggle against injustice without achieving anything except his own misfortune. While he, Fidel, who had done so much for the good of the people, whose works had instilled envy the world over, was hated and considered without merit. This would be the perfect revenge he could ever play on his detractors. In this world they would continue to try to denigrate him; in the other he would be untouchable.

When he returned, he found the devil, sitting cross-legged in the cold chair where J. E. Hoover had once sat, tapping his fingers on the table. He gazed at him naturally, as if they were old acquaintances at a scheduled meeting. 'It's just as well you came.'

Charming as ever, the devil replied beguilingly, 'Unlike others, I am always available when needed.'

'I have often been on the point of calling for you, so many afflictions have I suffered, but I have always managed to extricate myself on my own …'

'You know, you and I are similar. We have much in common. We started off as good-hearted angels who knew no evil – one obedient, the other already a little rebellious – until one day, knowing we were the most intelligent, we got fed up and decided to taste the pleasures of evil. From then on, so sweet are the delights of evil, there was no way back. However, your resistance surprises even me.'

'But I'm tired. I don't have the energy I had before, and I need your help to not lose the meaning of my life.'

The devil, who was pretty good at political intervention (the right placed him on the left, and the left placed him on the right, though he preferred the middle ground), stroked his goatee and gazed idly at the ceiling. 'Nobody knows this, not even you, but I have lent a hand to all the great leaders that have gone down in posterity, filling them with vigour when they wanted to give up, removing a powerful enemy from their path, ensuring that they received boundless affection from their people, and sometimes even from those they had conquered. So now it's your turn. Just ask what you want, and it shall be granted.'

Fidel stood a polite distance away, inhaled deeply, and took a serious look inside himself. Finally, he took a step toward the devil. 'In the future I want to be remembered as the man who confronted the tyranny of capitalism and rescued the people from exploitation. I want schoolbooks to describe the new society I built and for it to be compared with the previous one. I want my life to be studied, and, without hiding my mistakes, conclude that I did everything possible to give the men and women of this world a more worthy existence.' Now almost touching the devil, Fidel stopped speaking. He was exhausted, on the point of fainting.

'It will be done.'

'What do you want in exchange?'

The devil's lip curled and he rubbed an eye, amused at Fidel's naïvety. 'You have been making part of the payment for many years now. As for the rest, I'll be round to collect that after the battle, in which none of your men will come out alive.'

Hardly surprised, and knowing only too well who made the rules, Fidel was rebellious to a fault, even to the prince of darkness. Already imagining himself organising a mutiny among the condemned souls of hell, he dared ask an embarrassing question that had been niggling him. 'Don't take this badly, my dear devil, but what if God, by chance, decides to intervene in the battle as well?'

At this, Lucifer's horns, which till then had been hidden by his thick shock of black hair, began to protrude, the hairs on his body stood on end, and blue sparks began to fly from his eyes. Vexed, he got to his feet, overturning his chair, and stared furiously at El Comandante. Old doubts as to Fidel Castro's malevolence began to stir in him. Before disappearing the same way as he had arrived, with blood on his bitten tongue, he thundered a sarcastic retort that made the tent tremble: 'Just look at the world and tell me who is the strongest!'

At dawn, Fidel left the tent. He felt enormous peace of mind as he contemplated the growing light. Beyond heaven and hell, death was an uninterrupted, surprise-free, eternal sleep, the rest deserved after a life of struggle. No matter how powerful, no man could escape it. All are subject to the whims of its calling, often heard at the most inconvenient times. He, however, had escaped this frustrating fate. He had conjured it up so many times that he thought death had tired of looking for him, become fed up with the game, and understood that he, Fidel, would be the one to call death when he believed the time to be right. And that was how it was. Having already concluded his mission in this life, with nothing else left to wait for except deterioration and for everything he had built to return to dust, he decided to leave the stage feetfirst and to show death that even it existed to serve him.

El Comandante had become so serene, with death tamed and the end of life mastered, that while studying the rigid body of J. E. Hoover, with its contorted mouth and wide-open eyes, he didn't see a decomposing corpse. Nor did the pit into which they dragged Hoover in a bag appear to Fidel to be the final address of what had been a living being. He proved equally fearless, even relieved, when he was told that fifty of his soldiers had deserted during the night.

Varadero benefitted from this state of soul. The gag preventing him from pestering Fidel's ears and from inciting the soldiers to sedition was removed and total freedom of movement conceded. Still intrigued as to the reasons for the received kindness, he spotted El Comandante's face during the inspection of the troops and understood that a change had taken place. The insecure, tormented man that had arrested him now looked calm and confident, like someone who had just made a pact with the devil. Never had there been seen such an expression of inner peace in Fidel Castro. None of his masks looked like any of these. He recalled, after Fidel had overcome periods of great stress, he had looked more relaxed, but never entirely serene. He now appeared close to a state of ataraxia. For the materialist Varadero, who didn't believe in divine and diabolic interventions or those by saintly miracle workers, something strange had happened. And he became further disconcerted when, in the evening, they sent him to have a bath and a shave, as El Comandante was expecting him for dinner.

In Fidel's presence, Varadero experienced firsthand the mysterious change of mood responsible for them dining together. This was an honour never before granted and surely indicative of some terrible outcome, especially if you take the Italian nobility of the Renaissance, who poisoned their guests, as an example. Fidel displayed the vigour of a young man and the calm of an ascetic. His tone of voice never changed, and he didn't try to extract any information out of Varadero. He displayed a voracious appetite. The posture exhibited by El Comandante inhibited Varadero from talking, as if each word would be sacrilege, would defile a sanctuary. The confidence he'd built up since leaving the boat shrank to the point where he wouldn't dare to question El Comandante without being granted consent.

Once again he felt intimidated before the man who would decide his fate, unable even to make an attack at him in his thoughts. A drop of sweat trickled down his forehead, around his eyebrow, grazed his nose, and deposited itself on the corner of his lip. In its bitter taste, he found the enchantment of submission. If Fidel was once again showing the prime qualities that allowed him to command the revolution, Varadero became the humble worker, carrying out orders without discussion, in the belief he was serving his country.

Thus, he convinced himself that Fidel was preparing to humiliate him and teach him a lesson he would never forget. Fidel had always been like that, so why would he stop now? Allowing himself to be battered with guilt, he recognised that he had overstepped the mark, that he had exceeded it more out of the enjoyment of tarnishing El Comandante than for any other nobler reason, and, all things considered, he had proudly served the man whom he criticised so much. For the betrayal, for the effrontery, and for the opportunism, he therefore accepted the exemplary punishment that would be given to him. So, in the hope that it would all be over very quickly, he lowered his head, as if offering his neck to the executioner's sharpened blade.

However, Fidel no longer wanted to persecute anyone, and though he did not have any olive branch to hand out, he was also not armed with instruments of torture. Nearing the end of his life, ready to break through the tape on the finish line, adversaries and detractors behind him, he needed to open up to someone. And who better than Varadero to understand?

Fidel remembered the day they met, during the golden era of the revolution. He recalled the public excitement, thrilled yet telling of these events as if they had happened thousands of years ago. Caught up in this whirlwind of narrative, Varadero felt transported back to a distant past of which he retained few memories. Had it actually happened? Dazed by the vertigo of his own epic, he fell into free fall. In this journey through time, in a tunnel lit by the irresistible light that reality and fantasy produce when combined, after having revisited events that had moved them both, Fidel admitted that he would have done things differently in certain situations, but he didn't regret a thing. Unfortunately, the propaganda of the capitalist forces emphasised the repression and downplayed the progress of the revolution, putting him at risk of entering into the history books as 'another tyrant.' So, before a frozen Varadero, Fidel explained how such infamy would be avoided.

That night, Varadero left the camp. El Comandante, for reasons even the devil would not understand, had offered him the choice of dying with him or saving his own life.

A gentle breeze from the north blew on the backs of JFK and his soldiers, transporting them, in the form of odour, toward Fidel and his forces, which, facing the hill, received the first impact of the enemy through their nostrils. For Fidel's men the battle had started, attacked by an invisible strength that enveloped and penetrated them. Then the massacre began. Those who had arrived with fear became terrified. Those who were in control of their panic gave in to horror. Fidel confirmed his wildest expectations.

Before the raised terrain where JFK was waiting, he could see the military power of his enemy. The plan of honourable defeat, fighting against an army of greater numbers, could not fail. However, he needed to move the battle to a safe place, free of traps, and to hope, so as not to run the slightest risk, that the enemy decided to attack. As to the pact with the devil, he needn't worry, even though this was a hard task. After all, the devil was trustworthy in his own way. He also did amazing things, and never betrayed those who put their faith in him.

The problem for JFK, given that the pits would no longer work, was how to motivate troops into a brutal battle against an organised enemy, far different from the forces in disarray that had been promised. Nevertheless, even though he had the necessary skills for such a mission, with soldiers always ready to fight for fame and for wealth, for supreme ideals, or for the pleasure of killing, or for no reason at all, the certainty that countless lives would be lost now aroused in him an unexpected restlessness of conscience. At this time, he distanced himself from the soldiers and from the counsellor, as if isolation would bring him, if not the solution to the problem, then at least the indulgence for the act he was ready to carry out. However, as time ticked onwards and his resort to solitude slowly ran out, his inner turmoil continued to grow, taking on proportions hitherto unknown. What victory could ever justify the death of a human being?

In the meantime, Fidel, aware that any attempt to climb the hill would end in suicide, moved his army to an area further away, where he planned to await JFK's attack. Now all that was needed was for the enemy to collaborate, carry out its respective role, and respect the rules so he could finally engage in the final battle and end his existence with dignity. All things considered, he had to admit that this JFK, although he couldn't call him friend or comrade, was doing him an invaluable service. He had chosen the right man for an enemy. This great military leader, skillful diplomat, charismatic president, with whom, in other circumstances, he would have a totally different relationship, met all the conditions to lift Fidel to the status of martyr of the struggle for a fairer world. And in doing so, he would also acquire an enviable status: the man who killed Fidel Castro. It was, without a doubt, a great day for them both.

Fidel had slipped into a state of absolute calm. This didn't stop him, however, from wondering if the soldiers could sense, like animals taken for slaughter, their collective death. He would have liked to tell them that their sacrifice would not be in vain; that their death would honour a cause, a nation, and their descendants; that alive they were of little use, but dead they would be heroes. He would have liked to, but he couldn't.

The breeze picked up into a strong wind.

While he was watching the conceivable movements of the enemy, JFK associated the flight of J. E. Hoover with a deep distrust in the abilities of the nation to overcome its difficulties. When the surprise and shock had passed, unexpected like the sting of an insect, he tried to understand the reasons for such an attitude. He attributed this disbelief to the traitor's own insecurities. Maybe the same thing was happening with Fidel Castro, and behind the cool mask of the fighter there lay a worried and fearful man, who, using the war as a cover-up, was also fleeing from a reality he just couldn't face. Both of them believed they had uncovered an exit from the labyrinth in which they were trapped, breaking the darkness of the black suns illuminating them, to at long last hand themselves over to an explosive light that would end up blinding them.

The messenger, a frightened boy, had precise instructions as to what he should say and the way he should do it. Wielding a white flag hoisted above his shoulders, he descended the hill in a petrified state, heading slowly to his destination as if expecting the firing squad. Lost in the empty space separating the two armies, as if on a different planet, he did however establish a connection between the two, in which diplomacy would replace force. As he moved forward, distancing himself more and more from JFK and getting closer and closer to Fidel Castro, he feared he would forget his words. In a low voice he endlessly repeated his president's challenge to the enemy chief, ending each attempt with a different version.

At last, the messenger reached the front line of Fidel Castro's army. Seeing him so bewildered, the soldiers allowed him to pass without question. With the intrigued eyes of thousands of men locked on him, he was unable to see even one of their faces, his sleepwalker's vision blurred by the fixed image of Fidel Castro. Like a machine programmed for no other task, he searched obsessively for El Comandante, his wanderings finally halted by the appearance of his target, bursting out of his tent.

Ignoring the opinion of the generals, and without consulting the counsellor, JFK had charged the messenger with loudly proclaiming to Fidel Castro, before his troops, that he challenged him to a duel designed to avoid the death of so many men and that, in the event that he, JFK, won, the Castro soldiers would be free to choose their fate.

However, perhaps as part of the devil's game plan, the following words came out of the messenger's mouth, heard in amazement by the entire Castro army. 'Mister Fidel Castro, his Excellency JFK has instructed me to tell you that he accepts your challenge to single combat and that he promises to free your soldiers should he win.' Stunned by the page's statement, waiting a few seconds to see what this would mean, Castro's soldiers erupted in joy, bursting out in cries of 'Viva Fidel!' 'Viva El Comandante!' and also, though less convincingly, 'Viva la Revolución!' Perplexed, incredulous, tormented, Fidel poured invective on the devil and his mother.

Once back in JFK's camp, the messenger, relieved as if he had been saved from the death penalty, told the president that, having heard the message, they had all been so happy that they jumped for joy.

Fearing refusal, JFK, never beaten in a duel, was extremely satisfied that his negotiating skills had allowed him to save so many lives, and certain that victory would be his. Even so, every care could never be enough with this Fidel, this sly old fox with many more victories than defeats, and so he made sure to prepare for the fight, starting with sword practice.

The counsellor found him in these preparations. Suspicious that something was happening without him knowing, he tried, a little disrespectfully, to delve a little deeper. 'I beg your pardon, but what is this warming up for, seeing as Fidel is so far away?' Unperturbed, his eye on the tip of his sword, JFK philosophically replied, 'Why should the blood of my soldiers flow in these abandoned lands, if I alone can teach a lesson to the man who wants their blood to pour?'

The counsellor was astonished and took a while to work out the facts. 'Do you mean that even though you could watch the battle from a distance you are going to risk death once again in a duel?'

JFK took a swishing swipe right next to the counsellor before answering. 'In these times in which our people doubt their own abilities and at times seem to want to give up, it is vital that the person governing them shows with his own example that we can make it.' Confused, yet proud of his president, the counsellor retired discreetly. *Yes, we can!* he thought.

Fidel Castro's warm-up session was very different. In fact, he didn't undertake any sort of muscular limbering. The whirlwind of events had reduced him to a wilted plant, unable to move from the bed upon which he languished. There was no turning back now, nothing he could do to avoid his fate, no escape possible. The precipice was a step away and behind him the whole world was pushing. He felt like an old gladiator forced to return to the arena, after years of freedom at the expense of fierce fighting, for a final battle against a younger opponent.

Slaughtered while leading his men would be heroic; beaten in a duel, shameful. Overwhelmed, he stuck his neck off the side of the bed and expelled copious gushes of bilious vomit, as if he were made of nothing else. Would his body still be an impossible target for bullets? He then pulled out the knife he kept in his belt and, as if taking great pleasure in the act, slid the point of the blade across his wrists and his neck in a penetrating metal caress. Numb with ecstasy, he closed his eyelids and floated for moments disconnected from consciousness.

When he opened his eyes, any doubt had been dispelled. He was the man who feared nobody, protected by luck, by the gods, by fate, and he was going to kill JFK.

However, he couldn't help but request the devil's presence, so that he could explain this unexpected situation to him, quite different to the gentlemen's agreement they had come to. Nevertheless, as the devil is truly evil, or because he never grants more than one opportunity to anyone, or even because he exists only in the soul of every human being, Fidel received no reply.

Guided by intuition, Christ and Fátima approached the site of the battle, which ultimately would be a duel. After walking in circles, completely lost, through sheer luck – or perhaps divine intervention – they stumbled across JFK, high up, and Fidel Castro, down below at a distance. With eyes like a hawk, Fátima was the first to see the cluster of JFK's troops on the hill, and immediately signalled to Christ that he should crouch down. As there was nowhere to hide, not even a bush, he remained standing. He asked, 'So, aren't we going to talk to them?'

Silence.

They realised that they had not discussed the pacification plan thoroughly enough, with each of them concerned only with their own part in it – Fátima with the eclipse and Christ with the speech. After mulling over the consequences of this mistake, and hoping they still had time to sketch out a coherent plan that would make the most of both their contributions, they sat down exhausted on a rock.

The midday sun baking their heads had no idea of what would be happening to it. Could it be that, out of the blue, like a puppet of human will, the moon would be placed in front of it, and stop the earth from enjoying its luminous caress? How could the sun ever suspect that a natural phenomenon would be manipulated like a soybean, or a ewe, by a lady accompanied by Christ with the aim of creating dramatic conditions so that the saviour, in this second coming to earth, would pacify humanity once and for all? Even for the sun, which could produce a stunning aurora borealis and winds strong enough to destroy satellites, this was something difficult to swallow.

Explaining herself, Fátima felt compelled to give Christ a justification. 'I thought we had agreed that I would do the eclipse first and only then would the master enter the stage.' Christ became a little confused but, being the good Christian that he was, he quickly admitted that this had been the plan. Nevertheless, as if demonstrating that divinities always have the last word, he pointed out, with the seriousness of an academic adviser, some inaccuracies. 'Very well, but when will the eclipse take place exactly? How long will it last? How should I appear to them?' This shower of questions left Fátima speechless.

Christ then revealed that, the way he saw it, the eclipse should take place the moment the battle began (he was unaware it was a duel now) to catch them by surprise and should last no longer than a period of five minutes. Then the more complicated bit began. How should he appear to these bellicose beings, and what should he tell them? Arriving on a white steed, besides not having a horse (the donkey wouldn't do for such things), would be a little ridiculous, like a scene from a Bollywood movie. Falling from the sky or appearing out of nothing, like an apparition, was out of the question as he had already agreed not to perform any miracles. To arrive on the stage under his own steam to say to them, 'Peace on earth and good will to men,' seemed to him therefore the only smart move left, even if the eclipse never happened.

With their course set, all that remained was to wait for any sign that the battle had begun, a rush of people, roaring of voices, or roll of drums. They decided, however, to get closer to the probable epicentre of the battle, choosing a cornfield close by as the right place to observe the troops, to perform the eclipse and to use as a starting point for Christ's new epiphany.

While they were waiting, Christ opened up to Fátima. 'Guess what my father told me before I got here – That JFK was waging war in my name and that Fidel Castro took his inspiration from my principles. Both had been influenced by me, so I was to blame for it all.'

Fátima was appalled, and out of respect held back the 'Fuck!' on the tip of her tongue. She also managed to contain the phrase 'Utter nonsense,' also out of respect, this time for God, and found she didn't know what she should say.

Christ continued: 'I spent two sleepless nights because of this, endlessly mulling things over. It seemed really unfair to lumber me with responsibility for certain deviations of mankind. I do admit, though, that the matter disturbs me.'

Fátima, who in the meantime had made the problem her own, decided to speak up. 'JFK is a good Christian. He goes to mass every Sunday and gives alms, and so, in my opinion, I think it only natural that he invokes your protection when he goes to war.'

'But I have never sent anyone into battle. Anyone who can read between the lines will know I even forbade it.'

'Fine… but a war that can expand faith is not like the others. When the motives are good, it's almost acceptable.'

Christ frowned, amazed how his message could be distorted even by the purest of souls. 'Nobody has ever seen me at war, my dear friend. Peace, tolerance, and forgiveness are my only weapons. Blessed are the meek.'

Seeing that she had worked herself into a corner, and not daring to remind Christ that he had himself given a few slaps to the moneychangers in the temple, she attacked Fidel Castro. 'Look, the worst of the pair is without a doubt Fidel, as he believes he is God himself. He closed the churches, forced priests to work, and this story of building a society in which all men are equal is shameless plagiarism of your ideas, the result of which is very dubious.'

Christ listened to her carefully and took a while to respond, fearing that her condemnation of Fidel Castro contained a veiled criticism of him, thus confirming his father's theory. 'This Fidel had a very solid educational background... he seemed well intentioned, but then, as you would say, he ended up doing nothing but stupid things.'

Fátima, who detested any kind of revolution or change to the existing order, maintained her relentless attack. 'He was always a crook, a hypocrite. Why does he have a beard in that tropical climate?'

Christ then revealed his innate tendency to understand any kind of human behaviour, his ability to forgive, convinced that no man could be entirely bad. 'If he hadn't arrested anyone—'

'But he did, and he had them shot.'

'Sometimes, when I look at him, I think that my theories on equality among men are really utopian.'

'Don't compare yourself to this rogue.'

'You see, that's the problem. The majority of my followers aren't the best fans of equality and of sharing wealth. They prefer charity, and some, at the same time, argue the exact opposite, that each person should look after himself, that he who pays the piper should call the tune, denying entirely the essence of my thoughts.'

The image of some fervent Christians popped into Fátima's head, fans of the subjective interpretation of holy texts and of leaping moral obstacles. She returned to an awkward silence.

Christ digressed. 'Sermons on the mount, parables about the greedy rich and about rich youngsters, camels and needles – all for nothing.'

Fátima ventured some explanations and couldn't resist the suggestion. 'Some passages aren't all that practical, perhaps a little radical, and others confuse people. On the one hand, you feed the multitudes and on the other you throw pigs down ravines. Maybe you need to adapt them to modern times and explain that they don't need to be taken literally; otherwise you risk a lot of disappointments.'

'And what purpose would it serve if they only make use of what interests them?'

'Well, at least you save something.'

'And lose so much else…'

Disheartened, with the look of someone who has just found out what labour flexibility means, Christ concluded, 'For these reasons, I'm tempted to believe that the history of mankind would have followed the same path if I had come to earth or not.'

They were both engrossed in these meditations on human nature, divine responsibility, the guilt and innocence of both parties, having forgotten, and rightly so, to use the devil as an excuse or a scapegoat, when a rustle of footsteps over the grass interrupted them. And, like anyone caught doing something they don't want to be seen doing, they looked with embarrassment. Confusing them with local peasants, Varadero walked towards them in the knowledge he was among people of mild manners that only came to blows when dealing with issues of diverting water, crimes of passion, and football. As she had done a little earlier, Fátima repeated the order to crouch down, this time with military intonation. Varadero immediately obeyed the order and threw himself down onto the ground, crawling up to the pair as he had learned in military training camps.

In times of war you should never let your guard down, everyone is a suspect, and wolves wear sheep's clothing, so, quite prudently, none of them revealed their true identity.

'Who are you?' asked Fátima.

'I come from far away. I've come to visit an aunt.'

'And what is your name?'

'Vara, and you?'

'Us? I'm Fifa and he's José. We're brother and sister.'

Although none of them believed a word that had been said, they made out as if they had. 'Charmed,' they each said, as they already had enough problems.

Varadero deemed it wise to feign ignorance of the battle between JFK and Fidel Castro, questioning them on what was happening, using a shrewd technique that allowed him to avoid giving more explanations and which could provide clues about these two strangers. As they could not send him away, and the idea of tying and gagging him didn't enter their heads, Christ and Fátima looked at each other, without knowing what answer they should give. They needed to respond carefully. Eclipses and epiphanies weren't called for here. It would be better to act as if they were ignorant and illiterate. So, Christ, accustomed to facing opponents of a different calibre, took it upon himself to do the talking, incurring the complex task of creating a synthesis between the truth and hiding certain facts, without ever lying. 'There is going to be a terrible battle and many men will die if—' He almost said, 'we don't do anything.'

Varadero, a spy trained to detect the tiniest details in men's reactions, took note of the hesitation. 'If?'

'If common sense does not prevail,' Christ ended, wrapping his words in a fine smile.

'And is it not too late?'

Sitting next to Fátima and Christ, on the same rock, Varadero let his head fall into his hands, collapsing under the unbearable weight of an unforgivable deed. A fire lit in his stomach that threatened to erupt from his mouth, a private hell where he was already paying for the terrible sin. Before the setting of war, close to the leading actors ready for action, in the company of two secondary characters – or so he thought – he held himself responsible for the tragedy about to take place. Didn't he know that his attempt at dissuading Fidel Castro through logic or emotional pleas was doomed to failure from the outset? He knew it, but even so he had not lingered, as the pleasure of humiliating El Comandante had been more important than everything else. He could have killed him, but he had let him live to take delight in his misfortune. And now it was too late.

Nevertheless, as this wasn't a Greek tragedy of the type where there's plenty of sex and the atonement of guilt is really cruel, and as the conclusions of Varadero's troubled mind were excessively exaggerated, no divinity sadistically punished him. Quite the contrary.

Seeing him so contrite in his pain, bursting with torment and humiliation, more repentant than a wanton Magdelena or a crucified thief, Christ felt great compassion for Varadero's suffering. After all, to vilify was human, and to kill, equally human, was a much worse crime. And then, would one become a better man with remorseful self-flagellation? Does pain purify the soul or corrupt it for good?

He wanted to do something to alleviate the suffering, to soothe his anguish with some sort of balm, to free him of his demons and contain them inside pigs, but there weren't even piglets nearby. Nevertheless, how could he have done so without revealing to him that he was the saviour and had come once again to earth to redeem mankind, this time stopping the battle that bothered him so much, and that in this effort to save them, he would count on the collaboration of Fátima, the performer of eclipses?

He couldn't! Who would ever believe such a preposterous story? He hadn't returned to be confused with some lunatic or drunk. He had had enough of misunderstanding the other time.

For a while, he, too, so human once again, felt his blood boiling in his veins, an anger rising within him, and laid the blame upon Fidel Castro, regretting that they were no longer in the days of the Old Testament. However, his fury was short-lived, and he soon recovered his composure, as only defilers of sacred places greedy for profit made him truly lose his head.

Nevertheless, he couldn't just leave this repentant and confused soul adrift. He had a different mission. He had committed to not resorting to his array of supernatural powers, but he was before a man crippled with guilt, some of which was his responsibility. Fátima was right in a way, certain things should be explained in a different way, with an eye to how times and customs had changed. Then, with great tenderness, he placed his hand on Varadero's shoulder.

Having repeatedly reviewed the movements and blows he would carry out to beat Fidel Castro, his muscles had warmed up, and JFK left his tent armed only with a sword, immediately entering the gaze of the thousands of men waiting for him. Thus, captured under the anxious glare of his subjects, now floating in his dilated pupils, he multiplied into an army of great presidents, each of them presenting a unique characteristic, carved by the personality of the observer. In the peace emanated by a look devoid of hatred and in the relaxed actions of effortless movement, the counsellor saw a warrior that couldn't be defeated.

With countless JFKs burned onto the memory of the soldiers and commandants, the original turned his back on them and headed down the hill towards his destiny. If courage is defined by contempt for one's life, he was void of it. But, if such an attribute comes from mastering fear and the duty to face what threatens us, then JFK was a brave man.

The wind that had intimidated Fidel Castro's troops now pushed JFK onwards, as if urging him to continue. The president moved with the gracefulness of a great cat that already sensed its prey. Behind him lay the invisible wake of history.

When he reached a place that was of equal distance between his army and that of the enemy, he came to a halt and plunged his sword into the ground. The sun lit him from the side, projecting a timid shadow that escaped from his left flank. In this motionless position, JFK became the pointer on a sundial formed by the area of the plain, where the growth of his shadow measured the passage of time. Each minute that passed magnified and deformed it, producing a shapeless creature that was screaming, louder and louder, for Fidel Castro.

But Fidel didn't come.

In the meantime, the clamour of anxious voices grew among the Castro soldiers, struck by the vision of JFK and his shadow, in a prelude to rebellion. Inside El Comandante's tent, the commotion rang the bell that announced the moment of execution to this condemned man. But he was the executioner. Then he rose from the bed, regained his balance, and stuffed a pistol into his trouser pocket. If he had had a mirror, he would have been frightened by the image it reflected. When he came out, none of the soldiers saw that he was there, their backs facing him, mesmerised by the magnificent figure of JFK. As Fidel Castro passed through them, dragging himself towards his rival, he was like a stranger that nobody noticed, as if he no longer existed, incorporeal. Behind him lay the invisible wake of history.

At this moment, having realised what was about to happen, Fátima concentrated as hard as she possibly could on trying to bring about the eclipse. Varadero repressed the inexplicable urge to run to the aid of his commandant. Christ watched on undisturbed.

For the first and last time, Fidel Castro and JFK stood face-to-face, separated by mere metres. They were so close that they could look right inside each other. The first saw something that stunned him; the second saw nothing.

Finding him without a weapon in his hand, JFK walked away from his sword, tacitly accepting a fight with bare hands. He assumed Fidel preferred a short bout of boxing – this noble art in former times, a violent art today – from which would come out a victor but not a victim, or so he thought. JFK felt no relief. But at least one muscle in his face relaxed. With or without weapons, like all experienced fighters, he would wait for Fidel's onslaught, and once his opponent's offensive intentions had been revealed, he would defeat him with a lightning counterattack.

However, Fidel, unaware of any other way of fighting, assumed JFK was hiding a firearm, just like the mercenaries that tried to kill him.

Then, focusing on JFK with dull eyes, Fidel suddenly pulled out his weapon and fired it. But the bullet didn't hit its target, which had disappeared in an earthward dive. While Fidel was preparing a second shot, JFK hit him on the head with a stone. The impact of mineral against bone let out a muffled sound, which the torrent of blood diluted and extinguished. Fidel's arms dropped, his neck fell, and he collapsed. Now they were both on the ground – JFK lying face down, supported on his right hand, Fidel Castro fallen on his back, head hanging over his left shoulder.

In the distance, Fátima increased the pressure of her fingers on her temples: 'Move, moon, move!'

Varadero cried, 'Comandanteee!'

Christ observed the scene undisturbed.

JFK then got up, filled his chest with air, and pulled his sword out of the earth.

At this moment, soldiers and commandants of both armies launched into an unrestrained gallop, some down the hill, others across the plain, all desperate to witness the death of Fidel Castro. As if pulled by this torrent of people, Varadero left the cornfield and ran wildly, tripping, falling, and then getting up, in an attempt to save the life of El Comandante.

With three steps, JFK reached Fidel Castro, who was prostrate on the grass. The shadows of the two men melted into one of strange contours, and the sundial stopped working. JFK looked down at him. Blood plastered Fidel's hair. The blow to the head was deep but not fatal. His breathing had changed. He then slowly lifted the huge sword high above his head, as if wanting to purify it in the sky, and let loose a succession of deft blows on Fidel Castro.

When Varadero reached Fidel, throwing himself on the

inert body, he didn't recognise him. El Comandante had no beard. He was shaven to perfection.

At this moment, very slowly, as if ashamed, the moon began to languidly place its belly over that of the sun.

Note on the text

The reader who is aware of the history of the Cuban revolution has surely noted the origin of the name of the character Camilo Ochoa, resulting as it does from the combination of Camilo Cienfuegos and general Arnaldo Ochoa, two heroes of the revolution who accompanied Fidel from his guerrilla days in the Sierra Maestra all the way to taking of power. The former died in a plane accident in 1959 and the latter – who fought in Angola and in Ethiopia – was executed by a firing squad in 1989, accused of drug trafficking. Opposers of the regime state that they were both killed for having opposed Fidel Castro. In the case of Camilo Cienfuegos, they stress that his plane has never been found, along with the mysterious deaths of various people who could have explained what happened. Nevertheless, nobody has yet managed to prove Fidel Castro's guilt.

Various investigations into this matter have always led to the same result: if the anti-castristas can guarantee that their evidence is irrefutable (resorting to statements from dissidents such as Juan Orta and Huber Matos), impartial historians, with lack of proof, have been able to conclude nothing.

Camilo Ochoa is a fictional character.